The Spinster

Worth the Wait

by

Carol Jeanne Kennedy

Publication Rights

Cover: *Madame de Pompadour (Girl in a Blue Dress),* 1875-1880, by Edoardo Tofano (Italian, 1838-1920) Public Domain.

Dedications

To all my wonderful friends and family who helped me along the way in writing my novels. This book is dedicated to Don Knight, Billy Miller, Jean Gess, Carol Silvis, and Mary Burdick. Also, special thanks to Hennie Bekker whose musical compositions *Algonquin Trails* and *Stormy Sunday* provided the creative spark for *Winthrope*, followed by the rest of my Victorian Collection.

Other Great Novels by this Author

Winthrope – *Tragedy to Triumph*
The Arrangement – *Love Prevails*
Bobbin's Journal – *Waif to Wealth*
Poppy – *The Stolen Family*
Sophie & Juliet – *Rags to Royalty*
The Spinster – *Worth the Wait*
Holybourne – *The Magic of a Child*

Visit the author's website for exciting new additions: Her *A Novel Victorian Cookbook* with authentic Victorian cuisine that her characters loved to eat; the author's **hand-painted slipcases** to house the collection of novels, and a gallery of **her own paintings** inspired by 19th-Century artists.

Links and Reviews

Visit the author's website: KennedyLiterary.com
Like on Facebook: caroljeannekennedy
Follow on Twitter @carol823599

Table of Contents

Chapter 1 – There's a Divinity that Shapes Our Ends [1]

"I beg your pardon, Mr Duffy," cried Lizzy leaning out the window, "but, can't you see my revered roses?"

Squinting, the old crossing-sweeper tipped his crumpled hat. "Beg pardon Spinster Doddridge, but I'm half blind anymore."

Lizzy slammed the window shut with a thud. "Spinster Doddridge, indeed." Glancing at her sister, she fretted, "It wasn't so long ago, Emily, that one thought of a spinster as one who spins. And here we are *not* spinning, and yet we are regarded as spinsters."

"I would hardly think that anyone should call you a spinster at seventeen, Lizzy, nor I at twenty." She glanced at her sister's open book. "I take it you are reading another love story? Hmm, *Madame Bovary*, is it?"

Lizzy snuggled their cat, Mimi, to her neck. "But haven't you wondered why gentlemen never seek us out, Em?"

"You are ugly, and I am plain."

"I am quite serious, Em."

"Oh, stop fretting, Lizzy." She set aside her sewing. "I have a feeling you will fall head over heels very soon."

Tossing Mimi to her perch, Lizzy folded her arms, sighing deeply. "We simply must change our course."

"Lizzy, need I remind you every time you toss Mimi to the wind, her claws rip the sofa."

"Oh, who cares about that, Em, when we should care about finding a proper husband."

---

[1] Shakespeare, *Hamlet*, Act 5, Scene 2.

"And take up orderly housekeeping? Sharing our worldly goods?"

Lizzy plopped down in her chair. "Ouch." Reaching beneath her, she brought out a crumpled *Madame Bovary*.

Emily smirked. "*She* would know what to do."

"I do not think we are that desperate yet." Lizzy took in a weary breath. "Oh, were it not for the kindness of Uncle, we should starve."

"You are very right, dearest." Emily shrugged. "Short of hanging a "for sale" sign around my neck, I am at a loss as what more to do about it."

"Come along with Lady Mary and me tomorrow on our afternoon ride. You know very well Regent Park is the place to be seen."

"Hmm, Lady Mary, now there's one for you, a sheer glass of nothingness if there ever was one."

"You know very well we need her connections—if we are to find just the right sort of husband."

"A lot of good she has done you so far, Lizzy dearest. No, I think I shall not ride tomorrow. Besides, I do not like borrowing their horses, they are much too skittish. Thank you, but I shall remain here, spinning."

"Very well, Em, but I shall not, and from now on I will not leave the house looking like a dowdy old thing anymore. Indeed not." Lifting her chin, she huffed, "I shall wear my finest dresses, smile all the more, and flirt outrageously. I swear it."

"Indeed." Emily shook her head. "Perhaps then Lady Mary may supply you with another scandalous book to add to your reading repertoire."

* * *

The next afternoon as Lady Mary guided her mount into Regent Park, she hesitated. "Miss Lizzy, look there, it's Lady Charlotte with her nephew, Lord Swarthmore and his bride." As the Swarthmore's sauntered past, Mary cupped her mouth, "I hear his lordship is a beast of a husband."

"A beast?" Lizzy drew back. "Dear me, Lady Mary, one would hardly believe it. Why he looks all gentlemanly and dresses so fine."

"Humph," she held her hat as a strong breeze kicked up, "one never knows *beforehand* Lizzy."

"Well, I aim to find a suitable husband *beforehand*, Lady Mary." She tucked a loose curl behind her ear. "And one perhaps for Emily."

"Two? Oh, you silly thing," she scoffed. "What is suitability after all but good fortune." Tapping the whip to her hand, she added, "Indeed, I knew from the beginning Roger and I were ill-matched, but Papa needed his financial security to enhance his own. You must know that happiness in a marriage is really luck after all."

"Luck?" Lizzy stiffened. "Why, Lady Mary, it will be nothing of the sort for me. Have you not heard the old Arabian proverb: 'Cast a lucky fellow into the Nile, and he will come up with a fish in his mouth.' [2] Now that is luck. But I assure you, my idea of finding the right sort husband has nothing at all to do with luck."

"Oh, Miss Lizzy, you are such a ..."

Suddenly a dog came from out of nowhere and scooted between the hooves of Lizzy's mount, yelping and snapping. As her horse reared, Lizzy struck her head on a tree limb. Knocked unconscious, she landed face first atop a hedgerow, narrowly missing the spiked wrought-iron fence.

"Oh, dear God." Lady Mary slid from her mount. "Lizzy, Lizzy."

The only other sound being the flap of Lizzy's fancy petticoats as they fluttered in the breeze and a few gasps and murmurs from the passers-by. She remained motionless—her face buried in the hedge.

"Oh, dear me, someone, please help!" said Mary.

Shouts from the driver of a nearby carriage broke her cries, "Whoa! Whoa!" The horses' hooves skidded on the uneven stones as a gentleman leapt from the carriage. "God in heaven, madam, what happened?"

"A nasty little pug frightened my friend's horse, sir. As you can see, she was thrown."

"Dreadful thing, indeed." He took up Lizzy's hand. "I am a doctor, madam. Please, if you would move aside."

Dr Edward North, the prominent London doctor, was on his way to St. James Palace, where within the hour, he was to be knighted by Her Majesty, Queen Victoria.

"She has a strong pulse," he said.

---

[2] Arab proverb. Quoted from *Dictionary of Quotations* by James Wood (1893).

"Oh, thank God, sir." Wringing her handkerchief, Lady Mary nervously shuffled from one foot to the other.

Suddenly Lizzy's skirt began to billow wildly in the breeze, much like her inclinations toward life.

"Sir, whatever shall we do?"

"For one, madam, hold her skirt."

"Oh, but of course, sir."

Dr North shouted for his footman, Williams. "We must remove her from this bush." He lifted her head and grimaced. "Her face will be most untidy, I am afraid. I will take her shoulders, Williams, you take her ankles."

Grunting and groaning they successfully hoisted her from the bush.

"Gentle as she goes," directed the doctor.

"Aye, aye, sir."

Two policemen, all a flurry, hurried over. One held the intruding carriages back while the other thinned the curious crowd.

"I shall hold the door, sir," cried out a passer-by as he ran toward the doctor's carriage.

With great care, they situated Lizzy inside. Blood dripped from her forehead, cheeks and nose.

Straggling by, an old hag winced. "Hmm, 'er face looks like a cross-quilt, if you ask me."

"Doctor, I will hurry home for my husband and then straightaway to the hospital. Ah, to which hospital will she be taken, sir?" asked Mary.

"Victoria," he said reaching for the carriage door. "Do you know of her family, madam?"

"Oh, yes, sir. She has a sister ... and an uncle."

"Would you be so kind as to notify them?"

"Oh, indeed, sir, right away."

"Her name?"

"Elizabeth Doddridge. She is seventeen, sir." She found the doctor very handsome indeed. Waving her handkerchief, she cried back, "*Miss* Elizabeth Doddridge, sir."

He touched his hat and climbed into the carriage. "Thank you, madam."

Now groggy, Lizzy's eyes fluttered open. She gaped at the stranger sitting across from her. As her eyes focused on the blood splattered all over herself and the gentleman, she promptly spit up on the prestigious Dr North.

* * *

There had been a great commotion at the Doddridge Townhouse as Lady Mary, and her husband, Sir Roger Lennox, broke the news of Lizzy's ghastly fall to Emily. Holding tight to her husband's arm, Lady Mary related the horrid details of what had happened—the great commotion being the over-exaggeration of Lizzy's condition.

Sir Roger rolled his eyes as he pressed Emily's hand. "My dear, I assure you, your sister is in no danger. Why, she is in very capable hands with the distinguished Dr North." He gestured toward the door. "Come now, Miss Emily, use our carriage, your sister has been taken to Victoria Hospital."

* * *

After a few days of convalescing, Lizzy was sent home with a nasty headache and her head wrapped in what looked like a white Indian tarboosh. She assured Emily that she felt well enough to rest in the sunroom, and while she dozed, Mimi flexed her nails into Lizzy's turban. The fire in the hearth had prepared into ashes, grasped for a puff of red spark; a sudden tumble of wood and the doorbell startled Lizzy awake.

Nan, their nanny-maid since forever, answered the shrill ringer. "Miss Lizzy is not to be disturbed ... ."

Crouched behind her, Emily whispered, "Who is it?"

Nan swung the door open wide. "Just the Lennox's."

Emily's face blotched crimson. "Oh, oh, please do come in."

Lady Mary glared at Nan.

Sir Roger smiled. "Morning, Nan." He handed her his umbrella. "We don't mean to disturb Miss Lizzy."

Kicking the door closed, Nan frowned. "Indeed, she's been through a terrible ordeal and ... ."

"Nan, please," said Emily with a sigh, "just bring us tea, will you?"

"Very well, Your Highness."

Lady Mary's face soured. "Did I hear correctly?"

Emily gestured toward the drawing room. "Do come in, won't you?"

As Nan approached the sunroom where Lizzy lay, she stuck her head in the open door. "It's Madame Bovary and the fat man."

Lizzy groaned, "Shush, Nan, they will hear you." Trying to unhook Mimi's claws from her turban, she winced. "Ouch."

"I'll toss her out the window."

"No, no, you won't. And mind your manners with Lady Mary, Nan. You know how important it is that I find a husband. Ouch."

Lizzy lay back down, and within a short time, she heard the tinkled rattle of Nan's tea tray coming down the hall. She called out in a loud whisper, "And leave the drawing-room door open."

Emily stood at the window fussing with the lace curtain when Nan entered. "The late morning sun is all a-bright, I would say." She dropped the curtain. "Imagine with all this rain we've had of late that I should dare complain of such a thing." She returned to her chair and smiled at the Lennox's. "How silly of me." She turned to Nan. "Just set it there, Nan. I will pour."

"So, tell us, Miss Emily, how is the patient?" The rotund Sir Roger grunted as he scooted back into the cat's favourite haunt.

Nan, in usual fashion, clanged the tray atop the table, mumbling, "The patient is *trying* to rest."

Emily frowned. "Nan, please, just tend the fire."

"Indeed, do not disturb her on our account, Miss Emily," said Lady Mary as she grimaced at the cat-haired, shredded chair her husband occupied.

While humming, Nan poked the embers. "Nothing like a nice fire on such a day, eh?"

"The doctor stressed complete rest," Emily added with a polite nod to her guests. "But we do expect her to be up and about tomorrow."

"Well, then," said Sir Roger, "that is very good news, very good news, indeed."

"Oh, yes, up and about, surely that must be so." Lady Mary examined the tiny chip on the rim of her teacup, sighing. "But after I visited her in the hospital, why, her hands and face are so damaged." She returned the cup to its saucer. "Sorry to say, I am quite convinced that the chances of her now finding a wealthy husband are quite dim."

"Mary that's absurd." Sir Roger's double chin quivered over the smallish white cravat strangling about his neck.

"Not so very absurd, my dear," she corrected in a huff. "You wouldn't have looked at me twice if ... ."

"Absurd." Tea vapours meandered up his nose. "Absurd."

Nan stood behind Mary with her hands on her hips nodding along with Roger.

Pulling in her chin, Mary countered, "Absurd? Indeed not, sir. Let me explain how that prickly bush, in an instant, diminished Miss Lizzy's chances of finding the best sort of husband." She patted Emily's hand. "Skin you know, my dear. Flawless skin is the key."

"Mary," said Roger, "how utterly shallow of you. It's not just the skin that matters at all."

Emily hemmed. "But of course skin is important, but ..."

"You see, Roger, Miss Emily understands that I do not mean to be cruel. She does not find fault with me."

He stiffened. "I do not find fault with you, Mary, but for heaven's sake, Miss Lizzy's face is merely scratched. She shall heal. Besides, Dr North says the scars should be minimal."

"Oh, but, but even minimal disfiguration will look horrid," said Lady Mary.

"Horrid?" Emily's face crinkled in despair. "Dear me."

"Indeed, there was that particularly deep gash from her left cheek under her nose to the other." Mary shook her head. "No, no. I can not see any *wealthy* gentleman in our society seeking her out now." She clanked the silver spoon aside the saucer. "Imagine all those nasty red lines running helter-skelter all over her face."

While Nan cleared away the tea tray, she grunted, "Well, dearie, you've got that nasty gash between your lips, and it seems you've done quite well for yourself."

Sir Roger gagged, sputtered, and sprayed tea all over the front of his wife's sunny-yellow satin day dress.

Emily ordered Nan from the room. "And close the door behind you, Nan." She shook her head. "Do excuse Nan, Lady Mary. You know how the social graces lapse when they age. I assure you, I shall speak to her."

As Nan shuffled past the sunroom, Lizzy stood in the doorway shaking her head in disgust. "Nan, how could you? Now I shall never find a husband."

Continuing past, she shrugged. "Ring when you're hungry."

When Lizzy heard the Lennox's leave, she tugged on the rope pull.

Nan shuffled in with a tray. "Well now, a little bread with marmalade, my dear Lizzy?"

"You can't sweeten me after your outrageous behaviour today, Nan. No, you will not make me warm to you."

"Indeed," she set the tray on Lizzy's lap, "but this marmalade is for special occasions."

Lizzy glanced at the treat. "Special occasions, humph. You're impossible, Nan." She reached for the sweetened slice of bread. "Mmm, my head feels as if it will explode. By the way, where have you hidden my hand-mirror?"

Just then Emily bustled in. "Dear me, you're lucky enough to have a head."

Lizzy glanced at her hands. "Along with Nan and my bloody face, I shall be doomed to this house for the remainder of my life."

"Indeed you will," agreed Emily. "Nan, you know very well not to insult Lady Mary. However, shall Lizzy find a husband without her most excellent guidance?"

Nan huffed, "Indeed, husbands, what are they good for but for making dirt." She shooed the cat off the marmalade jar with her elbow. "Mangy little monster."

"Nan, must you?"

"Yes, I must." She lifted the tray and started for the door. "I have much to do today besides picking cat hairs from the jam."

"Much to do? What could you be so busy about?" asked Lizzy.

"Uncle Henry is due in today, dearest," said Emily. "And we must ready his room."

"Oh, yes, I had forgotten." Lizzy stood. "Well, then, I shall join everyone at the table for dinner this evening. There is no need waiting on me a moment longer."

"I don't think that is such a good idea," said Nan nudging Mimi toward the door with her foot.

"Hush now, I am recovered enough." Lizzy folded her quilt. "Put the tray away Nan, and then come help me dress."

* * *

Later that afternoon as Lizzy sat in the dining room awaiting Emily and Uncle Doddridge, she sighed deeply. "I'm still a bit weary, Nan. I pray Uncle Henry wasn't offended that I didn't greet him at the door this morning."

"Oh, not at all." She glanced at the mantle clock. "He and Emily should be down shortly. We told him about your fall, he understood."

Dabbing her lips, Lizzy lifted her head. "What was that?" She looked around the room. "Dear me, did I hear a meow?"

"No," said Nan as she settled the tureen on the sideboard.

"Why, I'm most certain I did. Nan, you didn't toss Mimi out the window again, did you?"

There, on the window ledge looking in sat Mimi. "Meow."

When Nan opened the window and cooed for her to come, the cat hissed, scrambled over her shoulder, and scratched her way beneath the sideboard.

"Well, the ungrateful little monster," said Nan brushing cat fuzz from her shoulder.

Lizzy heard the doorknob squeak and sat up. Her hat lay atop her head, crumpled and drooping toward the soup tureen.

When the door opened, Mimi dashed out. "Goodness me," said Uncle Doddridge steadying his cane, "what's troubling the cat?"

Nan shrugged. "Hates rain, I suppose."

Emily shook her head. "You've been up to no good again, Nan." She took uncle's elbow. "This way, dear, you will sit next to Lizzy."

"Indeed." He shuffled to her side. "Well, well, Niece, I missed your usual happy greeting upon my arrival this morning." He rubbed his eyes. "Elizabeth, what are you wearing on your head?"

"Her funeral hat, Mr Doddridge, sir." Nan exchanged glances with Emily. "Thinks she'll startle you if you see her face."

With his cane, he lifted Lizzy's veil and winced. "Nan told me about your nasty spill." He dropped the veil. "Ghastly."

Lizzy gasped. "Uncle!"

"Niece," he chuckled, "I am happy to find you alive."

She exhaled heavily. "Yes, Uncle Henry, I suppose I am as well." She removed her hat and tossed it to the floor. "I glanced in the mirror this morning, gagged and promptly called for my funeral hat." She buried her face in her hands and sighed. "What man shall ever look at me now?"

"There there my dear," he assured her, "what are good looks after all but clear skin? Oh, I wish I had only such a face to overcome my woes."

"I beg pardon, Uncle, for I am nothing compared to the loss of dearest Aunt Lucille, forgive me."

He lowered his head. "I miss her so."

Nan pulled out his chair. "Here we are now, Uncle Henry." She brushed a few crumbs from the seat. "Your place, sir."

He rested his cane on the table and sat. His dry old bones creaked as he settled into the well-worn hardwood chair. "She was the best sort of wife."

Emily took up her napkin. "Oh, indeed, Uncle; we loved her so."

The sisters nodded in agreement.

"Very well, Nan, you may serve the soup." Emily pressed Uncle's hand. "You must come live here with us. Now that Cousin Lavenia has married and moved away, country life must be too lonesome for you. "

"Indeed, and Neatham Lodge is too far away," added Lizzy.

Emily fluffed her napkin. "We are a wee family, Uncle, we must remain close."

He clasped his palsied hands in prayerful assembly. "I agree Emily, but I had hoped you two would come to Neatham, for my sake. I am an old man. London is too noisy. I hoped to live the remainder of my life in the country—in blessed peace. Surely I do not have long."

Neatham Park, north of the small river Wey, was situated in the ancient town of Holybourne—Emily and Lizzy's ancestral home—where they had been raised, and where their mother and father were laid to rest.

At their father's demise, the estate was entailed to his brother, Henry Doddridge. After his brother's death, he took in Emily and Lizzy, and a few years later, Aunt Lucille took in another niece, Lavenia. When Emily and Lizzy came of age, they moved into their uncle's London townhouse. Lavenia remained at Neatham Park until she married Rupert Haworth.

Emily shot a quick glance to Lizzy. "Why Uncle, we hadn't thought of returning to Neatham Park."

"But," chirped Lizzy, "we could certainly entertain the idea. A little time here in London perhaps, and a little time in the country would suit us all quite nicely."

Uncle glanced up at the portrait of his brother, Alfred. "Your father was a good man."

"Papa was indeed." Emily joined his admiring glance. "So good he was to us all, Uncle Henry."

"Indeed, my child, he so loved Neatham Park, our beloved home place. I must soon return." His eyes teary; he half-pleaded, "And, my dear Nieces, you must accompany me, stay with me there until ..."

Lizzy hugged him. "But of course, Uncle. Calm yourself."

"We will never leave you alone, Uncle," said Emily.

He kissed Lizzy's cheek. "On your aunt's deathbed, she made me promise to bequeath all her jewellery to you both."

Emily dabbed a string of drool from his lip. "Now, now, Uncle, you are too concerned over Aunt's things. I assure you, sir, Lizzy and I are in no hurry to secure them."

"But Lavenia is."

"Oh?" Emily's face wrinkled confusion. "Cousin Lavenia?"

"Has she caused you worry, Uncle?" said Lizzy.

"Some worry." He buttered his bread, clanged his knife alongside the plate. "Lavenia used to be such a pleasant child. We tried to warn her not to marry that rake, Rupert Haworth, but," he sighed, "she would not hear of it." He swallowed his bread. With a weary shake of his head, he added, "Lavenia had always lamented about spinsterhood. Had to wear just the latest style; be at the best parties; quite the sophisticate."

Lizzy squirmed. "Indeed, Uncle, I have found that the pursuit of a husband can be quite costly." She lightly ran her fingertips over the tiny scabs on her face.

He patted her hand. "Let them come to you, dearest. When a lady is desperate, it shows."

"My sentiments exactly, sir," said Nan ladling soup into each bowl.

"Yes," he lamented, "Lavenia shone so in her brilliant yellow dress that she apparently attracted the wrong moth."

Lizzy shuddered in her own yellow dress. "How unfortunate for Lavenia, sir."

"Your Aunt Lucille and I were so disappointed. Rupert gambles and drinks far too much."

"So we have heard, Uncle." Emily sighed spooning into her soup.

"But, sir, surely poor Lavenia had no inkling Mr Haworth was such a moth," said Lizzy.

"Such a moth, indeed," said Nan as she placed a bowl in front of Lizzy. "Heard about him long before we got that troublesome cat."

"Troublesome cat?"

"Ignore her, Uncle," said Lizzy, "she's being impertinent again."

Emily blew over the steamy broth. "Uncle, we had no idea to what extent Rupert Haworth engaged in such activities."

"Rupert and Lavenia have been at Neatham Park for the past month. They left only yesterday for London, returning to Haworth House."

"But Uncle, I am confused. We thought they were travelling on the Continent? Rupert was to show her ... ."

His hand began to shake violently. He dropped his bread. "Lavenia told me they may lose their furniture for collections."

Emily gasped. "Collections?"

"Why, that is scandalous," said Lizzy. "Dear me, sir, poor Cousin Lavenia, what must be done?"

He closed his eyes. "Indeed, I fear she will become quite desperate married to that man. Your Aunt Lucille must have had a premonition, for she ... ." He hesitated, opened his eyes and shook his head. "Well, my dears, it is all quite impossible."

Both sisters glanced up at him.

His voice lowered, "During a private tearful conversation, Lavenia informed me that her fortune was no more."

Emily threw down her napkin. "No more? God in heaven, sir, her dowry was considerable."

"Why, five thousand pounds at least," said Lizzy.

His shoulders heaved. "And ... she is with child."

Lizzy buried her head in her hands. "Oh, darling Lavenia."

"Uncle, we must do something," said Emily.

"I cannot think of any conclusion." Tears pooled in his rheumy eyes. "Lucille would have known what to do."

"There now, Uncle." Emily kissed his brow and fussed over him. "Lizzy and I shall put our heads together."

"We will?" said Lizzy.

"We will." Emily nodded assuredly. "We will devise a plan, Uncle Henry. Do not trouble yourself another second, sir. Cousin Lavenia will not be left in the cold."

"Oh, my no, Emily, no, no, she shall not be." Uncle Henry's bony little body sunk deeper into his chair. "Nieces, there is something more. Some very important information before I ... ."

Emily rubbed his age-wrinkled soft pink hand. "Go on, dear Uncle."

"When at Neatham, I will have my attorney speak to you both."

"Very well, sir," she said with a nod, "very well."

"Is there something wrong, Uncle?" asked Lizzy.

He dabbed his mouth and slowly rose from his chair. "No, nothing is wrong my dears, just a few details to be sorted out. Now, if you will excuse me, I am really very weary."

Nan pulled his chair out. "Upsy daisy, sir."

He took up his cane and nodded to her. "I will lie down now."

Nan and the sisters helped him to his room. Lizzy and Emily covered his thin little body with their papa's old napping quilt. Each, in turn, kissed his brow and left.

"The room is cosy and warm, Nan. Thank you," whispered Lizzy as she eased the door closed behind them. "Dear me, I wonder what Uncle's attorney has to say?"

"His will. No doubt Uncle is leaving everything to me."

"You mustn't jest, Nan," said Emily. "We only have enough money left to live in relative comfort for a few more years, and soon with no gardener—I haven't the heart to ask Uncle for more."

"God in heaven, sister, how dreadful. How are we to help Lavenia with only pennies to our name?"

As the three entered the drawing room, Nan attended the fire. Lizzy found Mimi hiding behind the sofa and lifted her onto her lap. "Perhaps Uncle's attorney will speak to us in regards to Lavenia. Perhaps he had devised a secret plan himself; perhaps he wishes her to come live at Neatham Park as well—without Rupert."

"Hardly, Lizzy," said Emily, "she is a married woman you know."

Nan brushed soot from her hands. "Not for long."

"Not for long?" Lizzy looked puzzled. "Why, Nan, what do you know?"

"More than I can share with you two now."

"Nan, what do you mean by being so secretive? You must share with us what you know. How are we to help Lavenia?" said Emily.

"You will know soon enough."

Chapter 2 – Neatham Park

The very next week the Doddridge family and Nan were well on their way to Neatham Park. Nan's head bobbled on Uncle's shoulder.

Lizzy giggled. "Look at the two of them, one in tune with the other." She glanced out the window and sat up. "Wake, everyone, we will soon cross the Wey."

Nan squinted out the window. "About time."

Uncle continued to snore.

"Only a mile from Neatham Park now," said Lizzy as the horses thundered over the bridge. "It is such an ancient crossing."

"Indeed it is." Emily snapped open her fan. "Remember when Papa told us about the pilgrims passing over it on their way to Canterbury?"

Uncle coughed and sputtered awake. "Pilgrims, where?"

"We are but a mile from home, sir," chuckled Lizzy, "and there is not a pilgrim in sight."

"Uncle, I have been thinking of a plan this entire ride. Hear me out," said Emily with a sly smile.

"A plan?" he asked.

"Indeed, I shall write to Lavenia and invite her to Neatham for a visit—perhaps a month."

He rubbed his eyes. "And?"

She fanned her warm face. "Well, sir, to offer assistance in her delicate condition."

Lizzy nodded in support, but unaware of just what *plan* her sister hand in mind.

"Go on," he said.

"Rupert would not leave London—what with his position at Heathrow. He owes far too much to risk debtors prison."

Lizzy lifted her veil. "Indeed, then we just may wean Lavenia from Rupert?"

"Oh, I doubt that," said Nan smirking.

Uncle Henry cleared his throat. "Indeed, Rupert will not get another penny from me."

"Perhaps I am better off without a husband," said Lizzy with a deep sigh.

Nan patted her hand. "There's a girl."

"I do hope Rupert does not cause you more grief, Uncle," said Emily.

"Despicable behaviour," said Nan.

Lizzy's nose flattened against the window. "Look, one of the hounds has come to greet us, the clever spotted one."

Emily stretched and yawned. "I would gladly trade places. I could use such a run."

The carriage ambled up the long gravel-bedded drive, and when they pulled under the Great House's brownstone carriage-porch, Maxwell, Uncle Henry's butler, stood waiting. "Good afternoon, sir. The house is in good order, sir."

Doddridge nodded. "Very good, Mr Maxwell." He gestured to Lizzy and Emily. "Come along, Nieces—come along, Nan."

Emily glanced around the Great Estate's magnificent flower gardens—old-fashioned flowers to be sure: primroses, pansies, stocks. She took in the always well-kept lawns, green and low. Horses grazed in the north pasture; gardeners raked and puttered; the sky was grey-white; water trickled in the portico's stone fountain. "Ah, it is good to be home, Uncle." She picked a yellow rose that grew very near the door—she supposed it wanted to live inside.

Lizzy glanced up at the name Doddridge carved above the door. "Home, Em." Tugging at her gloves, she entered sniffing the air. "A bit musty, though."

Emily tickled Lizzy's nose with the rose. "Fussy girl."

They followed Uncle Henry up the ancient oak staircase. With an affectionate kiss, they bid him good afternoon, "Until dinner, sir," they said in unison.

Lizzy entered her old room, the cosy atmosphere wrapped around her like a warm blanket. *Indeed, it is as I left it.* There came a light tap at the door. "Come," she said.

The maids, Mary and Helen, entered. One carried a fresh basin of water and the other a bucket of kindling to prepare the fire. As they went about their tasks, Lizzy sat at the open window-seat and gazed about the lush pasturelands. From the north, she watched as a man, riding a white horse at full gallop, race toward Uncle's garden fence.

"Dear me," she leaned into the window seat to get a better look.

The horse jumped the old rose hedge with ease while his dogs yelped and scooted between its thickets. The stranger dismounted and left his horse to meander at will—the dogs followed alongside him to the stables.

Lizzy held her hand to shield the morning sun. "Who is that man, Helen?"

Leaning over her shoulder, she glanced out. "Dr North, our neighbour, Miss Lizzy. He acquired Tillyard Lodge last year."

"Really? A certain Dr North attended me most recently in London."

"Indeed, Miss Lizzy, with such comings and goings at the Lodge, why, we hardly know what to make of the old place anymore."

Lizzy lowered the curtain. "Humph, I should think him rather impertinent for riding so carelessly about Neatham Park, jumping this and jumping that."

"Oh, yes," Helen nodded as she poured the basin water, "yes, indeed, miss, very impertinent."

"Tell me, does he visit Neatham often?"

"Oh, yes, Miss Lizzy, every day."

"Every day?"

Mary poked the embers. "Dr North has bred his sire to your uncle's great mare, Phoebe, miss. The foal is due any day."

"Oh, but of course, now I remember Uncle mentioning it. How absent-minded I am." She continued to stare after Dr North.

Mary curtsied. "Will that be all, Miss Lizzy?"

"Just make sure Nan is attended ... you know, the best room."

"Oh, indeed, miss," replied Mary with a knowing smile. "She is there already."

Lizzy giggled. "Yes, I suppose she will have her way." Dipping her fingers in the water basin, she dabbed her face lightly and then slipped off her dress. She lay across the bed and stretched. "Mmm," she mumbled as she studied the portrait of her mother above the white stone hearth, *Mama, how we miss you, dear*. She fluffed her pillows, snuggled into them and fell asleep.

Hearing someone tiptoe into her room, she startled awake.

"Forgive me, dear, if I woke you," said Emily as she picked up a quilt that had fallen to the floor.

"What is it, Em?"

"Lunch will be served within the hour, or would you rather eat here?"

Yawning, Lizzy sat up. "I shall come down, I am famished, Em."

"After lunch, we should take the air. It will do us both a bit of good."

"Indeed, a little sunshine, a little breeze, we shall gather a little bouquet of wildflowers perhaps?"

* * *

When the sisters finished lunch, they stepped out onto the crunchy pathway and meandered, arm-in-arm, toward the garden.

Emily took a deep breath. "Mmm, just feel the sunshine warm our shoulders, Sister."

Lizzy affectionately tweaked her sister's nose. "I count six marks on your nose today, Em. There were just five freckles yesterday."

"She neglects her heart who studies her glass." [3]

"Always the philosopher, Emily." Lizzy shook her skirt. "Remember all the petticoats we used to wear? How heavy they were."

"How many things of Mama's did I sweep off the tables?"

Lizzy giggled. "Indeed, many."

As the two neared the vine-covered gazebo, Lizzy stopped short. "Look there at that hound, Em."

"Where?"

"The black one curled there in such awkward fashion." She pointed. "Just there by the hedgerow."

Emily took Lizzy's hand. "Wait," she whispered, "something's wrong with it."

---

[3] Johann Kaspar Lavater (1754-1801), Swiss theologian. Quoted from *Proverbs* by William Hardcastle Browne, 1901.

"I think so, too." Lizzy slowly approached the dog. "Hello, dear girl."

"Leave it, Lizzy. It must be sick."

The hound glanced up at them, whimpered then dropped its head back onto the grass.

"God in heaven, Lizzy, that's Abby, Lavenia's dog."

"You are very right, Emily." Lizzy gently moved the dog's legs. "I don't find anything, Em." But when she probed the dog's belly, it whimpered. "Aha, she must have eaten something rotten."

Jacob, the gardener, hurried over. "Oh, Miss Elizabeth, that's Abby, Mrs Haworth's dog."

"Yes, we know, but she left her behind?"

"Oh, no, miss." He knelt. "She'd never do that. It was Mr Haworth who insisted it remain behind—he hated the dog." He ran his rough hands over Abby's head. "She had puppies months ago. We believe Mr Haworth killed them."

Lizzy gasped. "Killed them? What a terrible thing to say, Jacob."

"I am sorry, Miss Elizabeth, but it is the truth."

Lizzy stroked Abby's limp body. "Poor dear, poor abandoned dear. I will help you, girl."

Emily frowned. "I don't think so, Lizzy. Its eyes look glazed, and that's not a good sign."

"Jacob, there was a doctor here earlier, a Dr North?"

"Yes, Miss Elizabeth."

"Fetch him immediately, will you?"

Abby lifted her head and licked Lizzy's hand.

"Her tongue is hot, Em." Turning back to the dog, Lizzy cooed, "It will be all right, girl." She rubbed the dog's belly. "I know it hurts, girl. I know."

Emily held the parasol over her sister and the dog. "Come, Lizzy, it is beginning to rain."

"I can't leave her here, Emily. If she gets soaked, she will surely die."

"Well, you will surely die if you get soaked."

"Then we shall have to move her into the house."

Emily sighed deeply. "But what will Uncle say?"

"I am most certain he will understand."

* * *

Lizzy had blankets laid down for the dog in front of the huge hearthstone oven in the side kitchen. "I do hope she is comfortable, Em."

Rumblings of thunder boomed in the distance. Patches of lightning zigzagged across the kitchen's white-washed walls. Plops of rain splattered against the thick bubbled-glass windowpanes, the wind howled down the chimney fanning the flames into a frenzied mass.

Emily rubbed her arms briskly. "Well, the poor creature will at least stay dry."

"Perhaps I might tempt her with a bowl of milk," said Lizzy.

"Indeed not," came a man's voice as he hurried past them. Rain splattered them from his drenched coat as he knelt down beside the dog. "Not until I examine the animal."

Emily took Lizzy's hand and pulled her back. "You are Dr North, then?"

"Yes." He ran his wet hands over the dog's body.

"It's her stomach, sir," said Lizzy.

Emily pinched her thumb. "Shush."

"She is very ill," said the doctor. "What has she eaten?"

"We don't know for certain, Dr North, but the servants think she has been poisoned, sir," said Lizzy.

"Poisoned?" He examined the dog's eyes. "Perhaps." He reached into his leather bag and brought out a vile of dark liquid. "If she will only drink this." Holding it up to the light, he shook it. "But it is very bitter."

Lizzy knelt by his side. "May I try to feed her, sir?"

"Very well." He moved aside. "She has recently had pups, I see."

"So we have been told, sir." Lizzy stroked Abby's soft muzzle. Kneeling closer, she whispered, "Abby, come now, girl."

The dog sniffed Lizzy's hand.

"Her breath feels very warm." She dabbed a little medicine onto the dog's tongue, but Abby drew back. "Dr North, may I add a little sugar to the potion?"

"Very well."

Helen dashed to the cupboard and returned with the sugar-bowl. Lizzy mixed the potion with a dab of sugar in the palm of her hand. "Come girl." She lifted the dog's head. "Come, now." The dog licked Lizzy's hand clean.

"Cover the animal with as many blankets as she'll tolerate. Keep her warm," he said. "Throughout the night."

Lizzy stroked Abby's head and murmured, "I will stay the night with you, girl. You will survive, dear girl. Indeed, you'll not die in my arms." She layered the dog with the blankets. "There now, that should do it." Shaking her skirt from rain, she glanced around. "Where did the doctor go?"

"I have no idea." Emily shrugged. "He watched as you fed the dog and the next minute he was gone."

"Hmm, what an odd man he is."

"Oh, dear me, Miss Elizabeth," said Helen, "why, he is not odd at all. My sister is a dairymaid at Tillyard Lodge, and she often tells me he is very kind."

"Well, he may be kind, but odd all the same."

* * *

Early the next morning when Nan, still in her morning robe, came into the kitchen, she found a stranger kneeling over Lizzy and the dog. She quickly grabbed a meat cleaver. "And who might you be?"

He stood. "I beg your pardon, madam, I am Dr North."

"Hmm." Squinting at the tall stranger, she ran her finger over the sharp-edged tool. "You better be." Her frazzled grey hair sprouted about her nightcap like spring grass.

"Nan, what is the trouble?" Lizzy sat up, rubbing her eyes awake.

"Just mind to cover yourself, there's a stranger ... ."

Lizzy stood and found the doctor standing behind her. "Oh, sir, excuse me, I didn't see you."

"Says he's a doctor."

"Oh, indeed he is, Nan. The very one who attended me in London."

"Humph." Nan returned the cleaver to the butcher's block with a sharp thud. Grabbing cook's apron, she wrapped it around Lizzy's shoulders.

The doctor returned his attention to the dog. Kneeling alongside her, he sighed and gently closed Abby's eyes.

Lizzy knelt alongside him, her face raw from the wool blankets; her morning hair matted and tangled. She ran her hand over Abby's silky black body. "She is still warm—the poor dear."

"She did not die alone, Miss Doddridge," with a solemn smile he glanced up at Nan, "nor unloved."

"Pity the poor creature." Lizzy kissed her fingertips and placed them on Abby's head.

Dr North stood. "The animal should be removed."

"I'll see to it," said Nan.

"Miss Doddridge, perhaps you would be more comfortable in another room."

Glancing down at the lifeless little body, Lizzy nodded. "Indeed, sir, I would."

When she moved to leave the kitchen, she was surprised that the doctor followed her. "Indeed, sir, this way." She led him into the drawing room.

As they stood at the hearth to warm from the morning chill, he glanced about her neck, her face and hands. "So, you are healing quite nicely, I see." He took her chin examining her face at every angle. "Perhaps a few errant scars, but then again, perhaps not."

Lizzy blushed, tears pooled in her eyes. "For a little while, I had forgotten about my face." She glanced down. "Thank you for attending the poor dog, and in such dreadful weather. You are more than kind, sir."

He handed her his handkerchief. "Because of *your* kindness, Miss Doddridge, the dog did not suffer."

She dabbed her cheeks and winced. "Ouch."

"So, tears still sting, do they?"

"Indeed." Lizzy forced a smile. "I just found the poor creature yesterday afternoon." She met his attentive gaze. "Why I attached myself so quickly to her, I do not know. Forgive me for troubling you, Dr North."

"Miss Doddridge, I am a doctor. To lend aid is no trouble, I assure you."

"Even to a lowly dog, sir?"

"If I were half as compassionate as you, Miss Doddridge, even to a lowly dog, I should consider myself the best sort of human being."

Nan and Emily bustled in and found Lizzy, oblivious of her dishevelled hair, crumpled sleeping gown, and blood-stained kitchen apron hanging askew over her shoulders.

Nan cupped her mouth, "Pray she doesn't glance in the mirror."

Emily hemmed. "I was just told about the dog, Lizzy. How dreadful, dearest." She kissed Lizzy's cheek and turned to the doctor. "The servants just told me you were here, Dr North."

"Indeed, I arrived just moments ago, unannounced, do forgive the intrusion."

"Oh, sir, there was no intrusion at all, sir."

Lizzy nudged her.

"Oh, do forgive me, sir. I am Miss Emily Doddridge. Mr Henry Doddridge is our uncle. We met at the hospital last month—when Elizabeth was thrown from her mount."

He nodded politely. "Yes, of course, I remember you, Miss Doddridge. Indeed, it was a most unfortunate circumstance in which to meet."

"Yes," Emily glanced at Lizzy's hair and tried not to laugh.

Lizzy frowned. "What do you find so amusing, Sister?"

Nan hemmed. "You will, of course, stay for breakfast, Dr North. I will have a place set for you."

Emily nodded. "Oh, indeed, sir, for you have been more than kind."

"Thank you, but I must be on my way." With that, he turned. "Good morning, ladies." He held Lizzy's gaze and with an instant's notice to her face, her tangled hair and bloody apron, he smiled warmly. "Good day." He left.

Lizzy placed her hand over her heart. "Dear me, what a sweet look he gave me. What do you suppose he meant by that?"

"He must find you, ah, thought-provoking," said Nan.

"What, a good word from Nan?" said Emily.

"Oh, indeed." Lizzy hurried to the window to catch a glimpse of the kind doctor as he rode away. "And to think he once saved my life."

"And, to think, you once threw up on him," quipped Nan.

Lizzy's face soured. "Oh, oh, so I did," she sniffed the air. "But a little, Nan, but a little." She pulled the lace curtain aside and glanced out. "There now, come see for yourself at how well he rides."

Nan and Emily exchanged glances.

Lizzy dabbed her face and glanced down at his handkerchief. "Dear me, he forgot this."

Emily put her arm around her waist. "Well, I dare say, he must have had a good bit on his mind to have forgotten it."

Uncle entered the room, gaped at Lizzy and rubbed his eyes. "Eh gads, Elizabeth, did you fall off another horse?"

"Why, Uncle, what do you mean?"

* * *

Later that week as Lizzy was teaching Helen flower arranging in the drawing room, Emily bustled in, her purple taffeta dress crinkling like fine paper. She stopped in front of the mantle clock. "Uncle will join us shortly."

"Are we playing cards, Em?"

"Aren't you going with us to Bentley?"

"Oh, I forgot about that." Lizzy pushed a few daisies deeper into the vase. "No, I think not, Em. The weather is holding quite nicely, and I would really rather walk in the garden."

"Well, you must not take a chill."

"Ready, Nieces?" said Uncle Henry as he pushed open the door with his cane.

"No, Uncle," said Lizzy, "I am going for a walk instead."

"Very well, Elizabeth."

Emily kissed her cheek. "Do not overdo it, dear, remember it was not so long ago you injured yourself."

Glancing in the mirror, Lizzy dabbed her scars. "How can I forget?"

* * *

Lizzy's funeral hat lay on her bed. "I am really very sick of you, and today I will not put you on my head." She took up her parasol, closed her bedroom door and descended the stairs. Once out into the sweet summer air, she took in a deep breath. "I shall first visit Mama and Papa's grave."

While she stood at their grass mounds, she prayed, "Bless you, Mama and Papa." Gazing into the cool blue sky, she inhaled deeply. "Emily and I do miss you terribly. We are here to help Lavenia, but then you no doubt know all about it."

Just then a black bird swooped down and landed on a branch very near her. It flapped its wings, chirped several times, and then flew into the stables. Lizzy watched in amusement as he returned and repeated his actions.

"Hmm, so you want me to follow you?"

Nan would laugh at her, tease her; she was not yet convinced of such possibilities of talking birds. Besides all that, she would remind Lizzy: 'It was not so long ago women were burned at the stake for believing far less.'

As Lizzy pushed open the stable's door, she took in the heavy scent of horse dung and raw urine. She stood for a moment adjusting her eyes to the darkness when Phoebe, Uncle's prized broodmare, tossed her head and softly nickered to her.

"Well, Phoebe, you are due any day, I hear." She stroked her long silky neck and glanced over the open half-door to get a better look. Just then the mare swayed and staggered back. Her huge belly convulsed.

"Goodness gracious, Phoebe, I believe you're time has come." Lizzy backed away. "I'll find someone to help you." Hurrying out into the yard, she shouted, "Hello! Hello!" She spotted the gardener. "Jacob, where is everyone?"

"Went into Bentley, Miss Elizabeth."

"Phoebe is ready to foal at any second."

"Oh, dear me." He pushed the flower-cart aside. "Oh, well now, well now," he sputtered, "I'll ride over myself and fetch Dr North."

"I'll stay with Phoebe, Jacob. Hurry along now."

"Indeed I will, Miss Elizabeth."

Lizzy hurried back into the stables and found Phoebe lying on her side, her tail whisked hard on the yellow-stained straw; her huge belly was now moving in waves.

"Oh, Phoebe, the doctor will be here very soon." She unlatched the stall door and entered, being very much aware of the dangers of being near a foaling mare. Phoebe nickered, her ears pinned back, she blew heavy from her mouth and nostrils.

"Easy girl," said Lizzy as she stepped over the straw bedding careful as a cat. "I am here to help you." She gulped. "But, Phoebe, I don't know much about it, actually, silly me."

Just then the blackbird flew in and perched on the half door, eyeing Lizzy and the mare. It flapped his wings and chirped.

"Indeed, blackbird, I am here."

His beady black eyes darted about the stall, and then he flew away.

Phoebe's breathing quickened. Her legs began to jerk and thrash. Now breathing heavily, white foam sprayed from her nostrils and dripped from her mouth.

Lizzy stroked the mare's sweaty neck. "Oh, dear me, Phoebe, it will soon be over. Dr North should be here any moment." She grabbed her own stomach, gulping for air. "I will stay calm, Phoebe." She wiped her eyes. "I will stay calm. They should be here soon."

The mare struggled, groaned, and grunted hard as more white foam oozed from her mouth and nose.

Glancing over the horse's body, Lizzy cried, "Oh, it's coming ... it's coming! Push Phoebe, push girl!"

The mare's huge belly convulsed as the foal's front legs and head broke from its sack—with a watery whoosh it slipped out and onto the warm yellow straw. Breaking from the watery film, the foal's little head wobbled, his eyes glazed and confused.

"Oh, what a beautiful baby, Phoebe."

The mare struggled, gathered herself into a ball and sat up. Then, with one awkward movement, she stood, shook off and nudged her foal.

Giggling, Lizzy kissed the mare's soft muzzle. "Oh, you have every right to be proud, Phoebe."

As the mare swung around to attend her foal, she accidentally bumped into Lizzy sending her face first into the muck. Desperate to be clear from the awkward mare, she crawled away, gaging. She knew well not to open her eyes.

"Oh, God in heaven, now what have I done?" She felt about her face and cried, "It's in my hair! It's ... it's up my nose." She wiped her mouth on her sleeve. Her stomach churned.

Dr North rushed into the stall. "I say, what a fine foal."

Lizzy's hands flailed wildly as she stumbled toward the voice. Bumping into him, she held her churning stomach. But too late, she lurched and splattered down the front of the doctor's fine green and yellow tweed waistcoat.

Aghast, Jacob backed away. "God in heaven, Dr North, such a putrid business."

North took Lizzy's hand and led her out of the stall. "Jacob, hurry and find some rags. Hurry now."

She was still stiff as a mummy and gagging as he sat her on the grooms' bench.

Jacob returned with someone's old knickers. "Beg pardon, sir. It's the best I could do at the moment."

Laughing, the doctor grabbed them. "Very well."

Lizzy stiffened. "What is the humour when I am dying?"

Carefully dabbing the knickers about her eyes, he chuckled, "My, but you have the most unusual way of getting into remarkable situations, Miss Doddridge."

Lizzy squinted, first opening one eye and then the other. Perusing the front of his ruined waistcoat, she shuddered. "Oh, Dr North, I beg your pardon, sir. I truly beg your pardon. I was—I was just helping Phoebe when I slipped."

"Edward," said a feminine voice from behind them, "whatever are you doing?"

"Caroline," he stood, "meet my patient, Miss Elizabeth Doddridge."

She eyed Lizzy. "Well, I heard there was an important birth, but who gave birth to whom?"

Lizzy straightened with indignation. "I was helping Phoebe, madam. She was in distress. As you can clearly see, I slipped."

"Apparently." Caroline glanced over at the sturdy, well-formed foal. "Very nice, Edward, very nice."

"I haven't had a chance to look him over yet, Caroline. I've been a little preoccupied." He dabbed Lizzy's chin.

Holding a handkerchief to her nose, she nodded. "I can see that you have, Edward."

"There now, Miss Doddridge, I believe you shall live another day." He hid the knickers behind his back.

"Thank you, Dr North," she said, ignoring his arrogant wife. "I shall take a closer look at the foal now."

"You'll venture another fall, Miss Doddridge?"

"I survived the last one, sir."

He chuckled. "Yes, I suppose you did."

When they approached the foal, he ran his hand down its legs.

Lizzy leaned in closer. "Are they sound, sir?"

"See for yourself." He took her hand. "Run your hand down his foreleg, like this."

She blushed at his nearness.

"Do you feel the strength? Do you feel any abnormal bumps? Do you see any sores or bleeding?"

"No, sir," she whispered.

"Speak up my dear, one can hardly hear you," said Caroline leaning into the stall.

"Now run your hand over his head, fondle his ears; look at his eyes; they are wide apart and intelligent, are they not?"

"Oh, yes, indeed, they are very wide apart." Lizzy kissed the foal's forehead. "I love him already."

Phoebe nickered in agreement.

"Well, it seems his mother approves of your fine opinion." Lizzy giggled. "No doubt it is because I smell like him."

"Edward, do come along. We shall be late," said Caroline.

He smiled at Lizzy. "I must be going."

Her eyes sparkled. "Thank you, Dr North—for the lessons."

"Thank you for alerting Jacob. It could have been a difficult birth."

She sighed. "It was a difficult birth. Indeed, sir, for us both."

Looking at one another, they laughed.

"I think we shall be good friends, Miss Doddridge." When he teasingly brushed a little something more from her nose, she spied the knickers.

"Dear me, sir, do you always use old knickers to dibble and dab?"

"Usually not my own, Miss Doddridge. His face was flushed as he took Caroline's arm. "Good day, Miss Doddridge."

* * *

Emily and Uncle Henry had just returned from Bentley, and as they were climbing up the back steps, Emily stopped abruptly and wrinkled her nose. "What on earth is that dreadful smell?" She set her package on the porch landing and glanced around.

Uncle Henry sniffed the air. "Eh, gads, Jacob must be spreading manure again."

"No, it's just me," said Lizzy walking up behind them.

"God in heaven, dearest, what happened to you?"

"I foaled." Lizzy climbed the first few steps. "Oh, but he's a healthy baby boy."

Uncle squinted toward the stables. "Phoebe? Phoebe?" he said with great excitement.

"Indeed, Uncle Henry. She is doing very well. And despite my appearance, I am doing very well. The foal is the finest Dr North has ever seen."

"Dr North is here?"

"Was here," said Lizzy, "but he had to leave."

He glanced toward the mews and glanced back at Lizzy. "I am afraid I do not understand all that I should. Please explain, Elizabeth."

"A little black bird sent me to Phoebe's stall, Uncle. I arrived just in time to send for the doctor and assist Phoebe." She glanced down at her filthy frock. "I suppose I am a little messy."

Emily held her nose. "A little?"

"I couldn't help it, Em. No one else was around. I entered the stall and ... well, I slipped."

Uncle poked Lizzy with his cane and chuckled. "Well, then, Dr North will forever be indebted to you, Lizzy. He has come every day to check on the mare. He's been fussing over Phoebe like a mother hen."

She smiled. "Indeed."

"Indeed." Uncle gushed. "Oh, I must see the little fellow myself."

"After dinner, dear." Emily took his arm. "You must first rest."

"Hmm." He grunted with a nod glancing back at the barn. "Very well, then. I suppose you're right."

As Lizzy fell in behind them to enter the house, Emily took up Uncle's cane and barred her entrance. Pinching her nose, she pointed toward the servants' entrance. "That way, missy."

* * *

During dinner that night, Uncle pushed back from his plate. "Elizabeth, Emily suggested that we invite Dr and Mrs North to dinner next Saturday."

Lizzy set down her fork. "Hmm, yes, I suppose we must."

"Well, even without my spectacles, I saw that sour look, Elizabeth."

"It is just that Mrs North seems quite the prig, Uncle."

Emily tapped the table. "Your manners, Lizzy, we are in Uncle Henry's home now, please."

"Excuse me, sir, but when I met her in the stables today, she seemed quite haughty, all in all." Lizzy lifted her chin. "And for no apparent reason."

He stroked his chin. "Well, I cannot very well invite him and not her."

"Indeed not, sir," said Emily. "We'll manage, eh, Lizzy?"

Holding her chin in the air, Lizzy nodded. "I shall be delighted to entertain her, sir." She drummed her fingers tips on the table. "Hmm, yes, while she sips her wine, I shall hold my breath until my scabs bleed."

Chapter 3 – Lizzy and Dr North

In preparation for the dinner engagement with the Norths that following Saturday, the servants at Neatham Park had all the furniture polished like glass. The formal dining room was festooned with ferns, sward-greens, and beeswax candles. Fresh daisies, lilies and apple blossoms twigs were arranged in the crystal vases. Aunt Lucille's finest Irish linens were spread about the tables; the family's heirloom china gleamed.

Emily stood admiring the table. "Mr Maxwell, the setting is lovely."

"Thank you, Miss Emily," he stood erect and proud. "I shall light the candles five minutes before the guests enter the dining room, rest assured."

"Very well done," she said with an assuring smile.

"Yes, ma'am." He nodded with a kind smile. "Your voice carries the very sound of your mother's, Miss Emily."

"It does?" She smiled warmly. "Well, I suppose it would."

"And every day you're looking more and more like her as well."

"Thank you, Mr Maxwell. That's comforting. She was a grand lady. I miss Mama very much."

"We all do, Miss Emily."

The yard dogs barked. "Well, the company must be coming, miss," he said, moving toward the entrance door.

Emily hurried into the drawing room just as the mantle clock struck eight. "Well, Lizzy, at least Dr North and his wife are punctual."

"Commendable." Lizzy yawned as she stood by the hearth rubbing her hands over the fire.

"What is that?" Emily spied a basket sitting on the floor next to Lizzy's chair, it was moving.

"Kittens, Emily. I just ... ."

The door opened, Mr Maxwell entered. "Dr North."

Uncle startled awake, sputtering, "Indeed." He grabbed his cane and wobbled to stand. "Welcome, Dr North, welcome to Neatham Park."

North scanned the room. When his eyes met Emily, he nodded. He then found Lizzy and smiled. He held her gaze until she blushed. He extended his greeting. "Good evening, Doddridge."

"Come, come, Dr North." Uncle steadied himself. "May I have the honour of introducing my nieces, Miss Emily Doddridge and Miss Doddridge."

Emily curtsied. "We have met, Uncle. Remember, dear, last week when the dog Abby was ill?"

Taking Emily's hand, Dr North nodded. "So nice to see you again, Miss Doddridge."

Turning to Lizzy, he took her hand. His deep black eyes glittered upon her. "I have met your niece, Miss Doddridge, sir, in London, in your kitchen, and most recently, in Phoebe's stall."

"Indeed, Uncle." Lizzy giggled, her face flushed. "I have a propensity to vomit whenever we meet."

Uncle Henry and Emily froze—their faces paled. Dr North gazed into Lizzy's mischievous eyes; a slight smile crossed his lips. "And I have a feeling it will not be the last." He gently released her hand.

Uncle Henry moaned and sank back into his over-stuffed chair and dabbed his brow. But he quickly recovered. "Well, well, then, I am happy to see you, Dr North. Do come and sit with me." He gestured with his cane to the chair next to him.

"Indeed, sir."

"Dr North," offered Emily, "a glass of sherry, perhaps?"

"Thank you, yes, Miss Doddridge."

"Mrs North could not come, sir?" Uncle Henry's face had regained its pink glow.

"I have no wife, Doddridge."

Lizzy sat up joyously. "That's very good news, indeed."

"I beg your pardon, Miss Doddridge?" He cocked his head toward her as if he hadn't heard correctly.

Emily poured Dr North a sherry and frowned at Lizzy. "The good news is we both shall sit across from you at dinner."

"Oh, yes," Lizzy followed behind her sister, whispering, "And I shall sit on his lap."

Emily handed Dr North his sherry. "Here we are then." She smiled politely. "Phoebe's foal is handsome indeed, sir."

Lizzy broke in. "Oh, indeed, he is, Sister." She beamed. "Sound and healthy."

The doctor nodded. "Indeed, sound and healthy."

"Are you to raise him for yourself, sir?" Lizzy opened her fan, thinking she was quite charming, lovely, all in all. Very much aware of his demeanour around her, it was in his eyes. And now to think he was not married. Why, she was almost giddy at the prospect.

He paused at her question. "No, Miss Doddridge, I aim to raise him for my fiancé."

Lizzy folded her fan taking a few seconds to gather her wilted thoughts, to pump up her twisted smile, but her teeth went dry. "Well ... well, at least she has an eye for horses, sir."

"I beg your pardon, Miss Doddridge?"

"That lady in the stables, sir—the day Phoebe foaled. Was that not she?"

"Oh, my no," he set down his glass, "that was my sister, Caroline."

Uncle hemmed. "Dear me, had I known, I would have invited her to dinner this evening as well, Dr North. Do forgive me."

"No need to forgive, sir. At present, I am alone. Caroline and her husband left for Halifax this morning."

"Some other time, perhaps," said Emily holding an empty smile, feeling pity for her deflated sister.

Uncle Henry cupped his ear. "What is that I hear?"

"I beg your pardon, Uncle?" said Lizzy.

His face puckered. "I hear something meowing—"

Raising his leg, the doctor found a kitten climbing up his pant leg.

Rushing to his side, Lizzy knelt at his feet. "Oh, sir, you have found my kitten." She giggled. "She somehow escaped the others in the basket."

Uncle's face withered. "Do excuse, my niece, Dr North—she is rather fanatical about four-legged crawlies."

After he pried the kitten loose from his trousers, he held it up. "Hmm, calico, it is my favourite."

"It is?" Uncle ran his finger inside his tight cravat and swallowed hard. "How fortunate ... for you, sir."

"Then she is yours." Lizzy puffed up. "But you must wait a few more weeks, sir. She is much too young to leave her mother."

He turned the kitten around this way and that examining its fluffy little body, and with uncharacteristic abandon, he teased, "Oh, but I cannot wait a few weeks." He shot a quick glance at Lizzy; his dark eyes poured into her soul, his breath caught. He closed his eyes. "However, I will wait."

Mr Maxwell entered. "Dinner is served."

* * *

Uncle and Emily stood under the portico torchlight and bid goodnight to Dr North. Lizzy had moved into the darkness and blew goodbye kisses to him.

"Well, the normally quiet doctor certainly warmed to you, Lizzy," said Uncle.

She snuggled the calico to her neck. "I know."

He shook his head. "Actually, I think he is quite fond of you, Lizzy. That's the most I've heard from the man since I met him. Why, he even smiled several times."

"I shall marry him, someday, Uncle." Lizzy sighed.

Emily scoffed, "I hardly think so, Lizzy. He is very much older than you, dearest. And besides that, he has a fiancé."

Lizzy shrugged as she watched his carriage amble around the fountain and down the London Road. "But certainly he is not in love with her."

Uncle Henry scratched his head and shuffled back into the house.

* * *

On the kitten's sixth week of life, Lizzy was anxious to deliver the kitten to Dr North. With care, she put the calico in her basket and went in search of her sister. She found her with Nan in the study. "Emily, I must have you go with me to deliver the calico to Dr North."

Emily stood at the window. "It looks like rain, Lizzy. I do not wish to get soaked."

"It always looks like rain, Emily. Come along." She pouted. "You used to love to walk, even in the rain."

Nan sat wrapped in her day blanket sipping tea. "Have one of the servants deliver it." She exchanged glances with Emily and snickered.

"You two must not tease me." Lizzy's face flushed. "You know very well how fond I am of Dr North. Please, Em, do come with me. I cannot go alone. It would seem most unladylike."

"What?" Nan set down her cup. "You worry about being unladylike? You know very well he has a fiancé, Lizzy. He will only break your heart."

Emily nodded. "Dr North is a busy man—he is probably not even home. Leave the calico on his front step. He will thank you later."

Lizzy glanced up at a patch of clearing bright blue sky. "Very well, then." She pouted while stroking the kitten's furry head. "I shall walk alone."

Before entering the woods, Lizzy waved back at the Great House. "I know they are both watching me—and giggling." She turned and entered the dark, cool woods and was soon out into a sunlit meadow. She trudged through the tall, moist field grass, climbed two fences, and finally gazed down onto the rooftop of Tillyard Lodge. "Lovely view, Miss Calico."

She sat in the wild pasture grass and lifted the kitten from the basket. "There you go, kitty." Sitting Indian style, Lizzy snapped up a sweet-william and teased the kitten with it. Closing her eyes, she inhaled the beauty of the day. "It is so wonderful to be alive." Suddenly an odd noise startled her. "Who's there?" She hurriedly put the kitten back in the basket and held her heart.

The noise came again, and she eased up slowly, preparing to run. *Whatever it was* was situated on the other side of the great oak only a few feet away. The hairs on the back of her neck prickled.

"God in heaven, what could it be?" Just as she grabbed the basket to dash away, she stopped. "Why, it is an animal's whimper." She peeked around the oak tree. "Oh, merciful heavens, it's a puppy."

As she inched closer, the dog snarled. "Easy, pup, easy."

Now growling and barring its little needle sized teeth, Lizzy halted. "Very well, I will not come closer, girl." She shushed the meowing kitten. "But, what is around your neck? Oh, I see, poor dear, a bit of rope ... why it is near grown into your neck." She backed away. "I'll be back puppy—with water and food."

She ran down the hill to Tillyard Lodge. Clanging on the doorknocker, she cried, "Someone, please hurry."

A manservant opened the door.

Sweat beaded on her brow. Panting, she asked, "Is Dr North in?"

"Yes," he frowned, looking her up and down, "but he is not to be disturbed."

"Is he napping?"

The servant gaped. "I beg your pardon?"

"Well?"

"Yes, miss, he is."

"Wake him. Tell him it is Miss Elizabeth Doddridge. Please hurry, it's urgent."

"Yes, Miss Doddridge, do come in."

Lizzy bobbled the basket to quell the kitten's meowing, but that didn't help. She finally settled the calico on her shoulder. Just then Dr North hurried down the grand staircase two steps at a time in his slippers, his hair dishevelled.

Lizzy's heart raced at the intimacy of his appearance, half dressed and handsome. She rushed toward him taking his hand. "Oh, doctor you must come with me. I have found the most ..." she handed him the kitten, "... Oh, the most heart wrenching, disgusting ..."

"Oh, dear me, yes, yes, but of course." He handed the calico to the butler, Johnson. "I must first put my boots on, Miss Doddridge. I shall only be a moment."

"Make haste, doctor, she may not have much time to survive," said Lizzy.

He hurried up the stairs, calling back, "Johnson, grab my bag."

The doctor and Lizzy hurried from the house. Lizzy pointed toward the hill. "Up there, sir, is the way."

"Very well," he said hurrying along while tucking in his shirt.

When they neared the place where the poor animal was snagged, Lizzy grabbed his arm. "Stop," she panted, "there," she pointed and cried, "there. Look at that pitiful creature."

North shielded his eyes from the sun and in disbelief, whispered, "A dog?"

"A puppy, sir, abandoned, if you can believe such a thing, left to die."

"We have run near a quarter mile, uphill in the hottest part of the day ... ."

"Notice her neck, sir." Lizzy dabbed her eyes with her sleeve.

"What?" He moved closer. "God in heaven, the poor creature." He set down his bag.

"She will not let us near, sir."

"Of course not, we are a threat." Squinting, he added, "She must have run away. It looks as if her tether became entangled in that tree."

"Oh, yes. Now I see." Lizzy tiptoed closer. "You are correct, sir."

The dog snarled, and Lizzy jumped back. "Poor girl, I will not harm you."

He dabbed his sweaty brow. "We must fetch food and water."

"Very well, sir. I shall wait for you here."

"No, you must remain with me."

Startled at his command and in a rare moment of silence, she nodded.

He caught himself. "I mean, Miss Doddridge, you must not stay here with that starving animal. Who knows what she will do."

Lizzy nodded, but she was not scared one bit over the dog's snarl. "Oh, indeed, sir, as you wish." She allowed his power over her with excitement.

They hurried back down the hill and had the servants fill a jug of water and prepare a portion of raw chopped venison.

Lizzy spied the small package and frowned. "That hardly seems enough, Dr North."

"She is half-starved, Miss Doddridge. If we feed her too much, too soon, she will become sick."

Lizzy nodded in awe of his most excellent knowledge. She touched his sleeve. "I am most fortunate in knowing you, sir— what with your healing hands, your kind nature, your most superb mind."

Embarrassed, he glanced away. His neck and face flushed. "I have only learned what any man could certainly learn."

"One cannot learn *heart*, sir."

"Hmm, so," he stammered, "well, then, come along, Miss Doddridge, we must move on."

Hurrying up the hill, Lizzy sighed. "Listen, you can hear the poor dear whimper from here."

"Late, on my balcony just evening last, I thought I could hear a wayward hound bay, but I had no idea it was this poor creature suffering."

"Oh, no, Dr North, of course, you didn't." Lizzy's step was twice that of his trying to keep up. "No one could have imagined such a thing, sir."

He laughed. "Do you know what I think, Miss Doddridge?" He glanced at her lovely profile, upturned nose, her facial scratches from the London accident still healing.

Panting, she replied, "What, sir?"

"You think too highly of me." He smiled. "I am human, you know."

A warm glow spread through her. "Sir, you did save my life. The least I could do is hold you in high esteem."

There was a long silence as she continued alongside him, so near him. She could easily take his hand and kiss it. She loved his easy informality, his thick black hair bouncing untamed in the sweltering heat, his cheeks red and ruddy.

"Well, then," he paused, "in that case, I suppose you have every right to."

They both laughed.

When they reached the dog, Dr North unpacked the jug. "Now to figure out how we can place the water bowl near enough to her without getting bitten."

"Toss a morsel to her left, and perhaps the diversion will give me time to set the bowl to her right, sir."

"Hmm," he nodded, "brilliant."

Lizzy smiled. *Yes, I suppose I am.*

"I must soon remove her collar, but I believe she will need surgery for that."

Lizzy filled the bowl with water and moved closer, it snarled. "Easy puppy, easy. The dog lunged at her, but reaching the end of the tether, choked back with a whimper.

Lizzy winched. "Oh, dear God, she is in great pain, sir."

"Do not show your teeth, Miss Doddridge."

"Do not show my teeth?"

"Dogs interpret teeth as aggressiveness. Now, I am going to toss another morsel to her left, stay alert. On the count of three, I will toss it. Then if you can place the bowl nearer her."

"Very well, sir." As Lizzy inched her way closer, she spoke soft, kind words to the dog, careful not to show her teeth.

"One, two, three."

The dog moved toward the morsel then stopped and turned back snapping at Lizzy.

"Miss," he cried, "do not move!"

She froze. The dog was now just inches from her, growling and barring her teeth, snapping. Spittle flew from her sharp white teeth. Lizzy forced a smile. "Easy girl. There now, drink some water, girl." She slowly poured water over her fingers into the bowl. She cooed, "Come girl. Dearest little pup, I am sorry someone left you here to die." Tears rolled down her cheeks. "Indeed, little one, come drink."

The dog suddenly stopped snapping. Easing up to Lizzy's outstretched hand; she sniffed it several times and then stuck her nose in the water. As the dog lapped up the water, Lizzy glanced back at the worried doctor. "Toss the dog another morsel, sir. She will not bite me now."

He tossed the dog a bit of meat—she gobbled it down.

"I need more water, Dr North. If you could come close enough to just hand me the jug."

He inched up behind Lizzy and handed it to her. The dog growled. "Easy girl," soothed Lizzy, "easy." As she poured more water into the bowl, the pup greedily slurped it up.

"I will pull you away, Miss Doddridge. Do not move in haste." He slowly inched his way up behind her.

Lizzy slowly stood. He put his hands around her waist. "Hold me, sir. I do not want to be ripped to shreds." She closed her eyes and smiled to herself. "Torn to pieces, sir." She leaned back into his arms.

"Indeed not, miss. I would not allow such a thing." He stood for a moment holding her and then eased her back until well away from the pup. He sighed deeply gazing down into her face. "You are the bravest woman I have ever met, Miss Doddridge."

"And you, sir, the most brilliant."

A dark shadow crossed his eyes, and she knew he was no longer in her spell.

Gently releasing her, he dabbed his brow. "I must return to London, Miss Doddridge."

"I know, sir ... ."

He slowly gathered the things they had carried up. Pausing here and there, he seemed in no great rush to leave. Indeed, she sensed that he was falling in love with her. All she would have to do is take his hand at this moment, bring him to her; kiss his lips. Bury her mouth into his; hold his body to hers.

"I will be gone for several weeks. I will have Johnson accompany you up here. I think it wise that you, alone, attempt to tame the poor beast—gain her confidence. Then I shall put her up in the stables."

Lizzy sighed in frustration. She wanted him to be the one to take her hand, bring his mouth to hers. "Rest assured, sir, for I would not do such a thing."

He looked puzzled. "Do not do what, Miss Doddridge?"

She smiled and dismissed her silly thoughts. "Why, surely not the stables, sir. The pup so deserves a warm bed, loving people about, with happiness and goodwill. And she will miss you, terribly."

"She hardly knows me, Miss Doddridge."

"She knows enough, sir."

He glanced at the pitiful dog as it lay curled beneath the bushes, panting. He ran his fingers through his hair and sighed. "Very well, Miss Doddridge, *when* you tame her, she shall have a place inside. Then I must remove that ingrown rope from her neck."

Lizzy smiled at the dog. "Oh, I hope the place inside will be as grand as this place is horrid, sir." She turned to him; hope sparkled in her eyes. "When you remove the collar, sir, may I help?"

"Help? Why, you would faint away at the sight, I am very sure of it."

"I assure you, sir, I would not."

He studied her for a moment. "Very well, then. *We* will remove her collar." Upon closer inspection, he held his chin in thought. "Do you suppose this is a pup from the dog that died at Neatham Park, Miss Doddridge? She is every bit a retriever, and a black one. Very much like the one that died. I recall her name was Abby."

* * *

Lizzy rose early the next morning, hurried to dress and hurried to Emily's room. "Wake up, Em. We have much to do today." She looked at her sister's empty bed in surprise.

Emily came from around her privacy screen.

Lizzy's brows lifted. "Well, you are almost dressed I see."

"Indeed, it is a rare day when you are dressed before me," quipped Emily.

Lizzy gazed out the window and rubbed her arms briskly. "Oh, I do hope it doesn't rain. We have four fields, a stream to cross, two fences to climb, and a very cross little creature to mend."

"I am up to the challenge, dearest." Emily pulled on her walking boots. "Rain or shine matters nothing to me." She stood. "Shall we go?"

Lizzy eyed her sister's change of heart. "You weren't so willing yesterday, Emily."

"Move along now." She affectionately pinched her. "I must see this half-mad dog you and Dr North are going to tame."

Lizzy's face lit up. "Dr North has kindly allowed me to call him Sir Edward."

"Do not tell me, Lizzy."

She blushed. "Indeed, Em. Oh, I cannot tell you how much I love him."

"Careful Lizzy, older men can be quite clever."

"He is intelligent yes, brilliant, actually, but clever, no."

They stepped out into the crisp, cloudless morning air. Emily took her sister's hand. "I love you, Elizabeth. Do be careful."

"How can I be careful, Em? It is too late. I cannot help myself. He has always been in my heart, in my blood. I see only him. I hear only his voice." She sighed. "When I am around him, I am always learning new things. He is like a wonderful, handsome ... encyclopaedia."

Emily laughed. "The worst kind."

The sisters meandered through wild little pastures, waded through streams, and jumped fences. Stopping to gather in the beauty of the morning, they giggled at their drenched hems.

"Oh, no matter, love, they will dry," said Emily.

"I am blessed to have you for my sister, Em."

"I should wonder." She tightened the blue satin bows beneath her chin. "I am such a dull person. Without you in my life, I would probably never giggle; never ogle over the oddest insects you bring home. I would never have loved the animals you dragged in, would not have learned to whistle, nor wish to speak to the birds. I would say if Dr North lets you out of his sight, he is not as encyclopaedic as you think."

"Is encyclopaedic a real word, Emily?"

"Does it matter?"

Lizzy smiled dreamily. "I suppose not."

"Oh, Lizzy, I have often wished I could be as spontaneous as you—how easy it is for you to simply love things; love a man so passionately so soon after meeting."

Lizzy pulled her bonnet off, outstretched her arms, and defiantly put her face to the sun. "Em, you must simply let it in."

Emily lowered her head, hid her face in the shade of her bonnet. "I cannot, Lizzy."

"Like all living things Em, at first one must take baby steps."

"Lizzy, heed my advice. There is a very good chance that he may not love you in return. You must prepare yourself."

She hesitated at the notion. "Then Emily, I will have loved for nought. I cannot undo what my heart has willed. I cannot ignore him; cannot ignore the passion burning in my body—it simmers there for his asking."

Emily exhaled with a great sadness of truth. "How fortunate for you, Lizzy. I do not have flames in my heart nor such desire in my soul. I think I shall never find a man to love—to evoke such feelings."

"Oh, nonsense, Emily, I think beneath that façade of sophistication simmers passion fit for a gigolo."

"Gigolo? Why a gigolo is a man kept by a woman, I think."

"Well?" She giggled. "Is that so bad?"

Emily blushed. "For shame, Sister."

* * *

Over dinner that night, Uncle Henry listened in awe as Emily repeated how she and Lizzy found the puppy still attached to the tree by a piece of rope.

"Uncle you would be simply amazed at the poor dog. Somehow her tether got tangled in a tree. Had Lizzy not accidentally found her, she would have rotted to death."

Lizzy gagged. "Em, please."

"Yes, well, excuse me Lizzy," turning back to Uncle Henry, Emily went on, "but, by the Grace of God, she was rescued by Lizzy and by mid-morning, eating out of her hand."

Lizzy nodded. "Soon, I shall untie the creature and take her to Tillyard Lodge for safe keeping. That will be her new home. Sir Edward promised."

"Sir Edward's house? Sir Edward, Lizzy? You call Dr North, Sir Edward?"

Lizzy set down her water glass. "Yes, sir, he gave me permission. And he shall address me as Miss Elizabeth."

He shook his head. "I cannot believe it. Why, Lizzy, he is one of the most influential men in London. One of the finest scientists ... just knighted by Her Majesty not so long ago. He is from one of the finest families in England—he associates with very few—barely speaks to me, for that matter. He has been working on a cure for the typhoid—dedicated his life to its cure."

Lizzy's jaw dropped. She exchanged glances with Emily. "Sir, I had no idea."

"But, Uncle Henry," said Emily, "Dr North is engaged to be married. Surely he is not so unsociable."

"Dr North is engaged in arrangement only, Emily. She is Miss Beatrice Bingham. Her father owns the pharmaceutical company that has the finest labs, finest scientists, and the finest money in which to aid the doctor's research. And, for that matter, I hear, she fancies him quite a handsome catch indeed."

"Quite the catch." Lizzy dabbed her eyes.

Uncle Henry looked from one to the other. "Dear me, have I said something wrong?"

* * *

Lizzy attended to the pup every day while Sir Edward was away. She tried to quell her love visions of a forever-after with him; happy days, babies, dogs, birds. But she soon buried her fancy visions of securing his affections; Emily's brutal discussions with her always brought her back to earth: 'He is too serious, Lizzy. He has his life's work. There seems no room for even a wife.'

Lizzy would argue that Miss Bingham was to be his wife.

"But Lizzy, in name only. Dr North has come into his ways, and it has been rumoured there will be no children. Come to your senses, girl. I am quite convinced he could not make you happy." Emily took her chin. "He has his work, dearest. Would you wish to kill his spirit and noble ambitions to find a cure for the dreaded Typhoid?"

She nodded in shame. "You are very right, Emily. I must stop this foolish daydream." Sitting upright, she clenched her fists. "Very well, from now on I will guard my heart against him, I promise." A pang of guilt washed over her. "I should be ashamed. I shall not interfere with his life's work."

"Are you that much in love with him, Lizzy?"

"Indeed I am." She sighed deeply. "I shall remain a spinster, I suppose."

* * *

Sir Edward was to return from London within the week, and Lizzy had to find a proper place for the dog at Tillyard *before* he arrived.

"Indeed, a suitable shelter, *inside*, as Sir Edward promised," she said overlooking Tillyard, the dog sat obediently at her side. "Well, girl, I suppose we must be on our way." She ruffled the pup's thick black hair. "Come away, now."

While clanging Tillyard's doorbell, she spied a lovely flowering rose and picked it for Emily. The door opened, startling her.

"Good morning, Miss Doddridge."

"Oh," she hid the rose behind her back, "so, you remember me, Mr Johnson?"

He sniffed the air. "How could I forget?"

"Hmm, well, Mr Johnson, I am looking for a room for this dear creature."

He looked down at the dog. The dog looked up at him and growled. "Well, it cannot stay here, miss."

"Oh, but she belongs here, Mr Johnson. We must find her a suitable place until Sir Edward returns."

"Sir Edward is aware of *it* coming here?

"Indeed he is. Why, he even promised to provide proper shelter once she was tamed."

Johnson exhaled in exasperation. "I suppose it is tamed, then?"

"Oh, at my very command, Mr Johnson."

"Very well, then. Do come in whilst I discuss the situation with the groom."

Lizzy led the dog into the vestibule. "Lovely furnishings, they were Lady Marlboro's, you know," said Lizzy admiring the décor.

"Lady Marlboro?" asked Mr Johnson.

"She sold Tillyard Lodge to Sir Edward."

"I was not acquainted with the former owner, Miss Doddridge." He turned to leave and glanced back at the pup. "Do keep it under control, miss."

The dog's lip curled.

Lizzy patted its head. "No worries, Mr Johnson. I assure you, she is under my control at all times."

He eyed her and the dog, shook his head and disappeared down a long dark hallway. Lizzy heard a door open and close. She sniffed the rose, knelt and whispered to the dog, "He's no doubt searching for a rope to tie you up."

The dog whined.

"Yes, yes, I know, but if I have anything to do with it, you won't be tied up ever again" She wrinkled her nose. "You are a smelly thing. Indeed, a bath is in order."

Hearing footfalls, Lizzy stood. The dog leaned into her skirt folds and growled.

"Right this way, Miss Doddridge. We have found a place for the animal."

She followed Johnson out into the side yard and immediately spied a magnificent glass garden house just to her right. Standing at the open door, she leaned in. "Oh, yes," she nodded approvingly, "this will do quite nicely."

Johnson stopped and walked back to her. "I beg your pardon, Miss Doddridge?"

She walked into the glass garden and gawked at its wonderful ambience. "Yes, yes, lovely." Lizzy knelt and nestled the dog to her neck. "Just what we had in mind, not dark and dank, not smelly, but light and airy." She took a deep breath. "Ah, indeed, lots of fragrant prims."

Johnson's mouth gaped. "Oh, no, Miss Doddridge, not here. Why, this is Sir Edward's private conservatory—where he raises his revered flowers."

"Roses," said Lizzy admiring them, "yes, they are my very favourite, too." She sighed. "I might have guessed."

Frowning, he corrected, "Really, Miss Doddridge, you cannot leave that beast here."

The dog whined.

"Mr Johnson, do not fret so. I assume all responsibility. The only thing this poor creature needs besides roses to sniff is a warm sudsy bath. Do bring me a tub, will you?"

He looked as if he had bitten into a lemon.

"And lots of warm water—lavender soap, if you please." She walked a few feet and stopped. "Right here," she said as she stood in a patch of sunshine streaming through an open window from the glass ceiling. "Place the tub right here."

* * *

While Lizzy held the pup, she directed the servants as to the precise location in which to place the large copper tub. "Here," she stood in the sunlight. "Right here on this glorious spot where the sun is beaming in from the heavens."

"Beaming in from the heavens?" Johnson glanced up at the heavenly window. "Oh, God, I'm not part of this folly."

"Very well, Johnson," said Lizzy, "you may now pour."

Lizzy placed pup into water and reached for the soap, but the dog squirmed free clawing frantically to climb out. "Now, now, pup, you must stay."

Johnson shook his head. "Perhaps she has an aversion to lavender soap, miss."

"Very well, pup. I am as determined to bathe you as you are to escape." She pulled her boots off and climbed into the tub. "I shall scrub you here, then. Johnson, when I say pour, you may rinse her. Make sure the water is still warm."

He exhaled. "Dear me, Miss Doddridge, I'm afraid you'll become drenched."

"Do not worry over the matter, Johnson. I assure you, I will not drown."

"Very well, miss."

Johnson stood stoic holding the jug, he looked as if he could spit lemons.

Lizzy lathered up the unhappy pup and began scrubbing its legs and tail—careful to avoid its neck. As she piled soapy bubbles atop the dog's nose, she and Johnson giggled.

The sharp, shrill voice of a woman pierced the water slosh, "What in God's name is going on here?"

Lizzy held tight to the pup. "Excuse me, I ... ."

The dour-faced woman glared at Lizzy. "Who are you? And what are you doing there?"

Johnson set down the jug. "Oh, dear me, I shall go and find drying cloths, miss." He hurried from the conservatory.

Lizzy climbed out of the tub, irritated at the lady's high tone. She assumed the lady to be *the* Miss Beatrice Bingham, *the* fiancée. Holding her nose in the air, Lizzy sighed, "I am Miss Elizabeth Doddridge, madam, Neatham Park. And you must be Sir Edward's mother?"

Miss Bingham's face reddened. "Indeed not."

Edward entered. "Miss Elizabeth, what's going on here?"

"The girl must be mad, Edward—bathing in her clothes. How on earth did she get in here?"

"Miss Elizabeth?"

"Oh, Sir Edward, Mr Johnson said you were not at home. Had I only known ... ."

"Yes, yes, we arrived just moments ago." He glanced back at Miss Bingham.

Lizzy giggled and wiped lavender bubbles from her nose. "Forgive me, Sir Edward." She looked down at the sudsy dog. "I found just the best sort of place for her here, but first realised she must have a bath."

A stream of golden light filtered down upon her head. She wiped her hands on her skirt. "I thought this the perfect place to bathe her, sir. I did not want her to catch her death."

Edward rubbed the dog's head with affection. "You have tamed her already I see, Miss Elizabeth."

"Edward?" Miss Bingham hemmed, "what is the meaning of this?"

"Beatrice, do come and meet my neighbour, Miss Doddridge—and the dog she rescued. Miss Bingham, Miss Doddridge."

Lizzy nodded. "Very pleased, madam." She glanced at Edward. "But, sir, she is *your* dog. After all, she was found on your land."

"Sir Edward?" Miss Bingham repeated at the familiarity.

Lizzy was younger, lovelier, livelier—and besides all those deadly threats, she seemed to sense the attachment Edward and she had already formed.

Miss Bingham softened her tone. "Hmm, I had no idea you were so well acquainted with your neighbours, darling." She moved closer to the dog and then suddenly drew back. "Dear me, what's wrong with its neck?"

"She will need surgery to remove some rope fashioned as a collar, Beatrice—it has become ingrown—nothing more is wrong with her."

"The poor animal was abandoned, madam." Lizzy hugged the dog. "I found her just in time." Her frock was now dripping and pooling on the floor. "Oh, dear me, I must wring out my skirt or," she giggled, "I shall float away." When Lizzy made motion to move, the pup jumped out of the tub scurrying to her side.

Sir Edward's eyes smiled. "She loves you already, Miss Elizabeth."

"Miss Doddridge, just what do you call the pitiful creature?"

Lizzy shrugged. "I haven't the slightest, Miss Bingham. Sir Edward must find a name."

Just then the dog shook off. Water and soap suds splattered everyone.

"Oh," cried Miss Bingham, "Oh, spare me!"

Edward brushed her off with his handkerchief. "Now, Beatrice, it is only a little water."

She sneered. "Filthy dog water, Edward."

Lizzy wrung out her hem. "There now," she said smiling at Miss Bingham, "I will pull on my walking boots and set off for home."

"Indeed." Miss Bingham turned to Edward. "Our company will be arriving soon, dearest. We must not have them find such an animal roaming about the halls. What should they think?"

Edward glanced around. "By the way, where the dickens is she?" He moved toward the door. "The pup was just here."

Lizzy dropped her boots. "Why, she was sitting right next to me, sir."

"Well, she didn't go out this way, the door is closed tight."

"Hmm," Lizzy glanced around with a shrug, "I haven't the faintest."

"There," he pointed, "Miss Elizabeth, you go that way, I'll go this way."

Miss Bingham huffed, "I do hope you find the beast before our guests arrive, Edward."

"Here girl, come girl," said Lizzy walking barefoot about the huge atrium. She neared some dwarf plum trees and marvelled at their size. Baskets of white-edged green ivy hung from above, their tendrils groping in mid-air toward the white lattice ceiling rafters. Nearby sprouted arched ferns of deep green swinging like a whisper from hidden windows; summer air wafting about the china pots that brimmed bright with red roses, their petals curling and holding moisture that pooled in the deeper shades of a new beginning.

Edward came through an arched open passage and shrugged. "She must be hiding."

Lizzy closed her eyes and took in the moist perfumed air. "Indeed, Sir Edward, this is a very beautiful place in which to hide."

"I am happy you find it so, Miss Elizabeth." He glanced down and chuckled. "I see that you are barefoot."

"Have you never walked here in your bare feet, sir?"

"Never," he whispered.

"Never?" She leaned over and kissed a budding rose. "Then take them off."

He blushed. "Look there," he took her hand and knelt down. "See for yourself who is hiding under that holly bush?"

She loved the feel of his strong, soft hand, sensing that he wanted to hold her hand and not let go, she returned his strength, swam in the warm sensation of his touch. *I love you, Edward.*

"But you cannot see her with closed eyes, Miss Elizabeth."

She felt her face redden, felt his warm hand. This time she would not let it slip away. Euphoric, she felt as if champagne was bubbling through her veins. "Sir Edward?" she whispered.

"Yes, Miss Elizabeth."

The dog wiggled in between them and broke the spell. Their grasp was now vacant, unnatural and cool; his touch, gone—the feeling gone. A sickening premonition iced her heart. *Yes, it must be this way.*

Sir Edward ruffled the pup's head. "Perhaps we should name you Holly Bush."

The terrible promise she made to her sister to not thwart his noble work sobered her. "Holly Bush? Oh, I love the name Holly, but certainly not Bush, sir."

"Very well, Holly it is."

"Oh, I love the name, Sir Edward. How clever you are." She snuggled the pup. "The name Holly is quite nice, I should say."

Though Lizzy revelled in the intimacy of the moment, she knew not to linger in his spell. "Well, I suppose we must go back now."

"I beg your pardon, Miss Elizabeth?"

"I suppose, sir, you must return to your fiancé. Your company is coming."

He stiffened. Defiantly shoving his hands in his pockets, he took a deep breath. "Holly must first see my pond."

"But sir, Miss Bingham and your company await you?"

"So they do." He gestured to move ahead. "Come along now."

Lizzy fought her exuberance at being singled out for his favour. She tried to convince herself that it was not her he wanted to remain with, but the company he clearly did not want to be part of ... including Miss Bingham.

She was guided along a long, narrow corridor with opaque, off-white windows from floor to ceiling. Moist grass carpeted her bare feet. "This is indeed a wonderful hiding place."

"I have never thought about it quite that way, Miss Elizabeth, but you are very right."

"Indeed, sir. This is where I would come."

"When at Tillyard I am in here a good bit. I think here, compose, read, and study here."

She could see his mind at work, his soft patient hands slipped easily in and out of his pockets. *I will not ruin his good intentions.*

He smiled down into her face. "Indeed, I suppose you could say I hide here as well."

"From whom do you hide, sir?"

There was a long pause followed by a sigh. "I suppose myself, Miss Elizabeth." He continued along the narrow path. "You like flowers and enclosed glass houses, do you?"

She bent down and kissed the dog's head and then continued slowly alongside him. "Indeed, but I have never in my life been in one this exquisite, ever."

"Prince Albert and I, and the Queen, strolled through here last summer. Albert loved it so. It reminded him of ..."

"The Great Glass Exhibition in London, but of course," she whispered in awe. "This appears to be a miniature."

"He and Her Majesty stayed here upon occasion—to escape the children for a day or two."

"I could well imagine."

He smiled. "Yes, Miss Elizabeth." He reached for the dog. "Allow me. She must be tiresome."

"But of course, sir. After all, she belongs to you." She handed him the tether. "I was beginning to think you were not fond of her."

"You quite mistake my emotions, Miss Elizabeth." He looked deep into her eyes. "I care very deeply for all creatures."

She flustered. "I, I am very satisfied that you have the best intentions, the best sort of emotions, Sir Edward." Gesturing with her hand, she added, "Who would not, who creates such beauty as all this?"

"Thank you, Miss Elizabeth, how very kind of you to say so. Come then, and see my pond."

He reached for her arm, but Lizzy hesitated. She was not convinced that she should allow him to touch her. Fearful she could not keep her word not lure him into her heart, she masked her emotions and fawned over a magnificent early bloom. "And you created this beautiful rose as well?"

He puffed up. "It is another one of my life's work, Miss Elizabeth."

"Why, in my entire life, sir, I have never seen one so delicate, so exquisite." She sniffed it. "Magnificent."

"It is my latest creation, without even a proper name." He paused. "Please allow me to name it in your honour, Miss Elizabeth. I shall call it Elizabethan Magnificus—Eliza for short."

"Eliza?" Tears welled in her eyes. "Mama used to call me Eliza."

"Is that so?" He nodded as if feeling very clever. "Eliza was what my father called my mother with great affection."

"Do they live in London, sir?"

"My no, Miss Elizabeth, they have passed away."

"And mine, sir. I miss my mother terribly. Papa died ten years ago. Mama could not survive without him and died of a broken heart a few months later."

"I have heard of people loving so deeply, though I have never met such a couple, except perhaps, Her Majesty and Prince Albert." Glancing back at the rose, he continued, "Yes, Prince Albert used to pick rose bouquets for her. He so adored her."

"Hmm," Lizzy's brow furrowed, "I have often wondered just how happy they really were—being an arranged marriage."

"Indeed, she loved him first off. It was later that they grew close."

Deftly snipping the rose, he tenderly handed it to her. "Miss Elizabeth, please accept Eliza."

She held the delicate rose to her lips. "I do not believe in arranged marriages, Sir Edward. All the money or prestige in the world would not persuade me to marry someone I did not love beforehand."

He stroked the pup's head. "Indeed, but Prince Albert and Her Majesty learned to love each other."

"Still, I could not do such a thing—the very idea repulses me."

"You are a young woman yet, Miss Elizabeth. Oh, full of high ideals, grand schemes ... ." the dog growled. "Very well, Holly," he half-laughed, "I shan't dampen your friend's great expectations."

Lizzy lifted her chin. "I could no more marry a stranger than kiss a worm, sir."

"Even if you could save a life—perhaps find a cure for a terrible disease—make the world a healthier place?"

"No."

He laughed. "I do not believe you, Miss Elizabeth. You are much too kind."

"Someday you will believe me, Sir Edward."

He drew back. "Come now, Miss Elizabeth, I much prefer giggles to worms." He let Holly go. "There now, run to your heart's content." He took her hand. "Come along now, Miss Elizabeth, to my pond."

Just a few feet ahead, they passed through the garden doorway and out into a tree-shrouded yard. They were surrounded by ferns, small trees in tubs, lush green shrubbery, rose bushes in bloom—pinks, reds, whites, yellows. The grass was a deep dark green, well shaven and lush.

Lizzy gently pulled her hand away and walked over the cool grass and giggled. "It tickles my feet." She came upon the pond. "Oh, am I in a dream? Did you think of this scheme as well, sir?"

A slight smile crossed his lips. He nodded shyly.

On one side of the pond, brownstones sat overlapped and craggy; thick dark green moss grew between their ledges. A smallish waterfall trickled over quad-stones. Vines grew on and around the dwarf-sized plum, peach, and apricot trees. Sweet-williams grew in purple abundance everywhere. Huge yellow vine roses climbed the sides of the garden wall, butterflies flitted about, stopping now and again to sip the water.

Lizzy closed her eyes and inhaled deeply. "Beautiful." Hearing music, she opened her eyes. "Am I in heaven?"

Edward glanced toward the Great House. "It is my heaven, but I really believe you are hearing the musicians tuning their instruments, Miss Elizabeth."

"Oh, dear me, we really must hurry along then, sir," she fretted. "I have made you late for your company."

"Do not worry over the matter, Miss Elizabeth." He gestured with his head. "This way, we shall return to the house this way."

She glanced down at her muddy dress and bare feet. "Oh, sir, I must leave the way I came in. I wouldn't want to embarrass you."

"You could never embarrass me, Miss Elizabeth. Come now, this way."

He meandered along the path stopping now and again to study the sky, smell a rose; all the while the musicians played, a cadence of voices sang out, and Lizzy became more anxious that he would be scolded by Miss Bingham for being late. When they finally reached the vine-covered arch attached to the mansion, Sir Edward lowered his voice. "Miss Elizabeth, you must promise to never divulge this secret entryway."

"Oh, never, sir, never," she whispered. "You have my word."

His eyes twinkled. "Very well, then." He gently pushed open the door. "This is the way."

When they entered the drawing room, Lizzy suddenly stopped. "Why, I remember this room when Lady Marlboro lived here, sir. My sister, Emily and I, used to play in this very spot." She pointed. "Mama and Lady Marlboro would have their tea over there." She glanced at his secret entryway. "Yes, that clever little passage was where Mr Marlboro would remove to smoke his pipe."

Then came a voice shattering the moment, "Edward," said Miss Bingham, "so this is where you disappeared to." She smiled at the pup and softened. "I must say *it is* an adorable hound, Edward."

He looked half-convinced. "I beg your pardon, Beatrice?"

"I said that the hound is adorable, Edward."

As Miss Bingham came nearer, Holly snuggled closer to Lizzy.

"It is yours, is it not, Edward?"

Lizzy glanced at Edward and smiled. "It is a *she*," Lizzy beamed proudly. "And she is quite fond of Sir Edward already, Miss Bingham—tomorrow he will remove her collar."

"Tomorrow?"

Edward nodded. "Yes, tomorrow, Beatrice. I have learned most recently that Miss Elizabeth takes great interest in all things regarding animals. And I was just about to invite her to join in Holly's surgery—merely to observe, of course."

Lizzy lit up. "Indeed, sir," she gushed, "I would love to."

Miss Bingham drew back. "Holly? Holly? What a stupid name for a hound. I shall think of another—one more fitting in our society." She frowned. "Imagine calling out for a *Holly*." Snickering greatly, she added, "What should our friends think?"

Lizzy snuggled the dog. "Well, I think it is a wonderful name, Miss Bingham."

Miss Bingham glanced at Lizzy's filthy dress, her mud-caked feet and smirked. "Of course you would, Miss Doddridge."

"Beatrice," interrupted Edward, "excuse us. I will see Miss Elizabeth out."

Lizzy moved closer to Sir Edward, kissing the rose he gave her. She met Miss Bingham's hateful gaze and returned it.

"Sir Edward," Lizzy smiled, "may I take Holly home with me this evening? I do not think Mr Johnson has prepared an adequate sleeping box for her."

"An adequate box in which to sleep?" Miss Bingham stepped between Lizzy and Sir Edward. "The animal must sleep in my room then. I shall prepare a very pretty place near the hearth. Depend upon it, Miss Doddridge, I shall spoil her to death."

Lizzy gasped. "No. Holly is not ready to spend the night in ... here, Miss Bingham." She gently tugged Holly and hurried out.

As Lizzy rushed down the hall, the music became louder. "Oh, dash it all, that's the ballroom, I cannot go in there." She headed back up the hall.

"Miss Elizabeth," Sir Edward caught up with her, "I must apologise."

"She may have the largest dowry in the world, the finest pharmaceutical company in all England, sir, but she will not, nor will she ever, have Holly. Excuse me, sir." She brushed by him, "I can see myself out."

Lizzy hurried away. Guests were coming toward her, and she turned down another hall. "Oh, dear me, where exactly is the front door?"

She tried to remember Tillyard Lodge from when she was a little girl, but with little success. She found a dim lit passage, walls festooned with old gilded portraits. "Oh, yes, this is the way."

She followed the passage to its end, tripping over heavy thick rugs, down endless hallways, past unfamiliar statues, when finally she stopped. "Oh, Holly, I am quite lost."

She sat heavily in a hall chair burying her head in her hands. Hearing footfalls, she hurriedly slipped through an open door. It was a magnificent room, where a nice fire crackled in the hearth. Suddenly the door opened, she closed her eyes and held her breath. Holly's body wiggled.

"Dear me, Miss Elizabeth, what are you doing in my study?"

She sighed in relief. "Oh, Sir Edward, it is you."

Johnson entered the room, found Lizzy and the dog, and not batting an eye, half-bowed. "Sir, the Binghams await you in the ballroom."

"Indeed, Mr Johnson. Bring two sherries, and Mr Johnson, a chop."

"A chop." He glanced at Holly. "Very good, sir" He bowed from the room.

Lizzy giggled. "A chop? How very kind of you, sir."

"Please have a seat, Miss Elizabeth."

Music from the ballroom filled the air. She envisioned him taking her up into his arms and waltzing about the floor. "This is a very elegant room, sir." She took in the scent of cherry tobacco. Taking a high-backed chair by the warm fire, she stared at the flames. "Forgive my rudeness, Sir Edward, but I believe Miss Bingham does not, nor will she ever, warm to me. In the future, sir, I will try and remain out of her sight."

Mr Johnson entered the room. "Your sherry, sir." He glanced at the dog. "Shall I tend the dog, sir?"

"I will, thank you, Mr Johnson," said Lizzy, and set the saucer full of meat near the hearth, and when the pup gobbled it up, Lizzy smiled. "Well, Sir Edward, now I really must be going. It is quite late. If you would but lead me toward the door."

Holly burped, and the two laughed.

"Thank you for showing me your most excellent creations, sir." Withdrawing the rose from her pocket, she sighed. "I shall press this and keep it always."

They both stood for a very long time in front of the hearth in silence. The fire crackled and hissed, Holly relaxed, curled into a ball and fell off to sleep. Music again filled the air. The mantle clock struck nine soft tones.

Lizzy's eyes glistened as she reached for Holly. "I really must be going, sir."

"Very well," he whispered, "if you really must."

"I must."

"Would tomorrow morning suit you?"

"To remove her collar?" Lizzy gently ruffled Holly's head. "Indeed, Sir Edward, I will be prompt." She smiled. "And I will try and remain out of Miss Bingham's sight."

"You must not concern yourself over the matter, Miss Elizabeth. Miss Bingham never rises before noon." His eyes clouded. "Come now, I shall have my carriage take you home."

"Oh, thank you, Sir Edward, but I would rather walk."

"But, it will be dark within the hour."

"I am not afraid of the dark, sir. Besides, the moon will be brilliant, the air brisk and sparkly, and if I am lucky, I shall wish upon a falling star."

"I could not allow such a thing, Miss Elizabeth."

She was a little taken aback. "Not to wish upon a star, sir?"

"That you should walk home alone, unprotected."

* * *

Lizzy entered the Great House of Neatham Park and upon finding Uncle and Nan sitting in the study, pulled off her gloves and kissed his warm cheek. "Good evening, dear Uncle, good evening, Nan."

"Lizzy," he said in amazement, "surely you did not walk such a distance in the dark?"

"I wanted to, Uncle, but Sir Edward would not allow such a thing." Whispering, "He is very much in love with me, I should imagine."

Nan sat in front of the fire and shook her head. "Silly girl. Emily has set off for Tillyard Lodge in search of you. She was very worried." Glancing at the floor, she gaped. "Is that a dog hiding behind you?"

Stepping aside, Lizzy smiled. "Oh, yes, Nan. This is the poor creature I found several weeks ago at Tillyard Lodge."

Uncle rubbed his chin as he eyed the rascal pup. "Is she safe, Lizzy?"

"Oh, quite, sir. She still trembles around people, growls now and again, but beneath her gruffness she is kindness itself—we are now quite certain it is one of Abby's pups, Uncle Henry."

"Hmm, well, if she is half as smart as her mother, you will have a great pet, Elizabeth. Retrievers are very good natured. Abby never left Lavenia's side." He shook his head. "She will be heartbroken when she learns the news of her demise."

The pup growled as Emily's carriage approached.

"Well now," said Uncle with a surprised look, "the pup does have her mother's instinct."

"Come Holly, we shall greet Emily. You remember her, you shall remember her." Lizzy stood near the torchlight as its flames slapped the late evening air. She waved. "Hello, Sister. Look, will you, at my prize. We call her Holly."

Moulding within the folds of Lizzy's dress, the dog barked.

"Dare I take another step and be devoured by the beast?" Emily held out her hand and called softly, "Hello, Holly. May I come into my home?"

Holly sniffed her hand, wagged her tail, and jumped up pawing her dress.

"You have been granted safe passage, Em."

"I just met Dr North, briefly." Emily removed her gloves and wrap. "I missed you by a quarter of an hour. How did you get home?"

"Sir Edward's carriage, the low road."

Emily nodded. "That's why we missed each other." She handed her wrap to Helen. "Well, I dare say, you must have made a huge impression on the doctor, Lizzy. Imagine having already secured his carriage."

She giggled. "Had you the fortune of meeting his fiancé, Miss Bingham?"

"No, but there were a thousand eyes on me all the while I waited in the vestibule."

"She does not let him out of her sight for a second." Lizzy laughed. "But we managed to elude her for a little while this afternoon."

"Lizzy?"

"Sir Edward took me on a tour through his atrium, or I should call it his crystal atrium. Oh, Em, it is one of the most beautiful, magnificent creations I have ever seen. It is a glass garden house—walls, ceilings—everything. Oh, very much like the one in London. Prince Albert and Queen Victoria strolled through it—stayed there just last summer. You must see his pond; his gardens, and his roses. Oh, God in heaven, Em, he named a rose in my honour." Pulling out the wilted flower from her pocket, she sniffed it. "An Elizabethan rose, Elizabethan Magnificus—in my honour."

Emily took her hand. "Careful, dearest, careful."

"He called it Eliza for short."

"Dear me, how tender."

"Oh, yes, he told me his father called his mother Eliza with great affection—her name was also Elizabeth."

Sadness spread across Emily's face. She took Lizzy's hand pressing it to her heart. "Lizzy, what about your vow to leave him to his life's work?"

"I did not weaken so much as to tempt him, Em. I have kept my promise."

"Oh, Lizzy, he has already broken your heart."

Uncle Henry clanged his way into the vestibule with his cane. "Ah, there you are my dear nieces. Come, I have a letter I must share with you two."

They followed him into the study where he took to his favourite chair by the fire. He removed the letter from a well-worn leather envelope and slid his finger under the seal.

Lizzy and Emily took to their chairs nearest Nan.

Uncle read the letter aloud:

"3 June 1870 – Upton House, London
Dearest Uncle Doddridge,

It pains me exceedingly to ask, sir. But I need assistance. Perhaps a hundred pounds would suffice. I believe I am very near those 'dire straits' you warned me about last month, and I fear I will not be able to feed the unborn—that which is growing inside me.

Oh, dearest Uncle, how right you were regarding Rupert—he is more than a scoundrel. After a particularly difficult morning owing to my condition, he left in disgust taking his clothes with him. I will post this immediately, Sir. I hope it finds you in health.

Your obedient and loving cousin,
Lavenia Haworth"

Emily shook her head. " 'Not be able to feed that which is growing inside me?' Oh, dear Uncle Henry, how dreadful."

"It is beyond dreadful, Emily. We must go to her, Uncle," said Lizzy, "at first light."

"Indeed, what a fool-hardy idiot of a husband." Nan shook her head in disgust.

Lizzy gently hugged Holly. "I must return her. She was to have surgery tomorrow morning." She sighed heavily. "And I so wanted to be there."

Uncle Henry patted Lizzy's head. "I believe the good doctor will be able to operate without your assistance this one time, my dear."

Thinking of Miss Bingham, her face soured. "It is not the good doctor I am worried about, sir."

"Oh?" He replied with a frown. "Why is that?"

Lizzy shook her head. "I will not complicate your life further, Uncle." Leaving the room with Holly in tow, she called back, "I am really very tired. I will see you all in the morning. Good night."

* * *

The following morning there came a tap at Lizzy's door.

"Come," she called.

Poking her head around the door, Emily yawned. "Time to rise. We will be leaving for London within the hour, love."

Lizzy sat in the window seat, gazing out. "I have been awake the night, Em."

Coming to her side, Emily hugged her. "You did not sleep the whole night through, Lizzy? Why? What is wrong?" She felt her brow. "You are not warm."

"I took Holly back to Tillyard Lodge, Em, earlier this morning. I left her with Mr Johnson, the butler. Poor soul, I woke him terribly early."

"And?"

"I left Sir Edward a note explaining that we had to leave for London immediately, an emergency and that I could not help him with his surgery."

"Oh, I suppose he will postpone the operation, then."

"This is no time to jest, Em. Without me being there, Miss Bingham will exert her influence over him and ..." Lizzy dabbed her eyes, "and in a fit of jealousy, she just may cause Holly great harm."

"Lizzy, surely she is not that wicked."

"Oh, but I believe she is very near that wicked—if not there entirely."

"Dearest, you are much too tender-hearted. I assure you Dr North will not let anything happen to Holly."

Lizzy wiped her eyes. "I pray you are right."

"Anyone who names a rose after a lady will do everything in his power to secure the affections of her dog."

"But Holly is *his* dog, Em."

"I really think she belongs to you both."

"Oh, Emily," she kissed her cheek, "how right you are. How wise and clever your mind works." She blew her nose. "I feel so much the better now."

"Indeed, come along, we must be on our way."

Standing, Lizzy grabbed her hat and wrap. "Hurry to London, hurry to home."

Chapter 4 – Lavenia and the Haworth House

London was dry, stifling with an airless swirl of stench. The street sweepers had not yet come, though it was late morning. Horse dung and house slop lay strewn about.

Nan shuddered. "This section of town was once quite lovely. Well," she pressed Lizzy's hand, "do wish Lavenia well for me. It will take me a few months to put the Doddridge townhouse back in its proper order. It is not good to leave the servants alone too terribly long, you know."

"Oh, indeed, Nan, how well we know," said Emily with a firm nod.

"But we will miss you, Nan," said Lizzy.

As the carriage pulled in front of the Doddridge townhouse, Nan stepped out. "Do not bother to come in, with such little notice the servants will be caught unawares," she cackled in apparent delight.

Uncle nodded. "You'll soon put things to right, Nan."

"Oh, indeed, sir." She stood straight and waved them off. "Good-bye now."

Lizzy leaned out the door and blew kisses to her. "I shall miss you!"

"Oh, silly girl, hurry off now, hug Lavenia for me," said Nan.

The Doddridge carriage moved into the crowded street and made way to the Haworth House, where Lavenia awaited them.

"She's peeking from the window, Uncle," said Lizzy with a sigh.

"Pretend not to notice." Uncle stepped from the carriage. "Watson, I shall ring the bell myself."

The door opened immediately. "Uncle Henry," Lavenia burst into tears, "do come in, sir."

He gestured toward the carriage. "May your cousins come in, Lavenia?"

Crying into her handkerchief, she nodded.

Emily took Lizzy's hand. "Very well, let us get this over and done with."

"Oh, Em, do you hear how pitiful she weeps; how thin she looks—her hair straggly and unkempt."

"Come along, Lizzy, Lavenia has always had such hair."

"Oh, yes, yes," she hurried behind her sister, "so she has."

Bustling up the steps, Emily added, "And she has always been skinny."

Lavenia stood at the open door motioning them in with her little white handkerchief. "Do come in, Cousin Emily and Cousin Lizzy. I would boil a pot of tea, but ... ."

"You are out of tea." Emily waved her off. "Lavenia, dearest, do not fret over such inconsequential ... ."

"Hmm," Lizzy interrupted, "such a big word, Em."

Lavenia laughed. "You two are quite the jesters. Come now, do let us go up to the parlour. At present, it is the warmest room."

Climbing the stairs, both sisters noticed the bare walls and exchanged glances. Once inside the tidy, but scarcely-furnished room, Lizzy squatted on the floor like a Turk. Emily escorted Uncle to the hard-backed chair by the fire. "Uncle, this is your favourite, remember?"

"How could I forget, my love." Sitting, he hung his cane off the bare, once cluttered mantle ledge. Glancing around, he sighed.

Emily and Lavenia shared the iron settee that had been brought in from the garden. There was little noise about the house, excepting the brattle of the hall clock.

"Well, at least you have the time of day, Lavenia," said Lizzy trying to be cheerful.

"Little comfort that, Lizzy," she said, looking sour. "I can get as much glancing out the window at the town clock."

"Now, now," said Uncle Henry, "it is only furniture, Lavenia."

"Hmm, yes, Uncle, only furniture until one must sleep on the floor."

He gasped. "Do not tell me, Lavenia, in your condition?"

She rubbed her back. "They took the bed just yesterday, Uncle. It has only been one night that I have been ... without it."

Standing, he grabbed his cane. "Well, there is nothing more for you here, Lavenia. You will come home with us this very minute."

Emily hugged Lavenia. "Well, here is some good news to cheer you, dearest Cousin. You will be happy to know that Lizzy rescued one of Abby's pups—nursed it back to health."

"Back to health?" She adjusted her shawl about her shoulders. "Why, how should you know of such a thing? Rupert was to see that they all found good homes."

The sisters exchanged glances.

"Oh," Emily stammered, "well, ah ... ."

Lizzy shrugged. "One must have gotten homesick, Lavenia. I found her while I was out walking near Tillyard Lodge." She smiled assuredly.

"Well, then, I am relieved you found only one. Abby had seven puppies, you know. Oh, how I miss her. Her sweet loving nature is such a comfort to me. I cannot wait until I wrap my arms around her once more." Walking to the window, she shook her head. "There is little else I have to look forward to, Cousin."

Uncle Henry steadied himself on his cane. "Well, we look forward to having you at Neatham, Lavenia."

"Oh, but of course, Uncle, how rude of me." She dabbed her nose. "Uncle, may I have a word with you?"

Emily took Lizzy's hand. "We shall wait in the carriage, Uncle."

Descending the stairs, Lizzy whispered, "God in heaven, Em. What are we to say about Abby? How can we tell her she died?"

"I will tell her when we reach Neatham Park. Surely Dr North will allow Lavenia to see Holly. That should cheer her."

"Oh, yes, dearest Holly. When I have not been praying for dear Lavenia, I have been praying for dear Holly—and that Sir Edward did not have any difficulty removing the rope."

Climbing into the carriage, Emily pressed Lizzy's hand assuredly. "I hear he is most excellent."

"From whom, Em?"

"Helen."

"Our Helen from Neatham Park?"

"You know how the servants gossip, Lizzy. They say he is a very serious scientist, and very generous."

"Oh, we have certainly been acquainted with his serious side, Em. And I am sure of his kind generosity, but … ."

Emily glanced out the carriage window. "Shush, here they come."

Lavenia paused before entering the carriage and glanced back at Haworth House. "Good-bye." Lifting her skirt, she stepped into the carriage.

* * *

As the horses clomped up Neatham Park's long twisted road, Phoebe and her foal ran willy-nilly alongside the white-fenced pasture.

Lavenia sighed deeply. "This is the very first, and no doubt the last, Great House I shall ever live in." Orphaned at twelve, her Aunt and Uncle Doddridge took her in. Emily and Lizzy enfolded her lovingly into the family.

"Look, Lavenia, do you see Dr North's foal?" Lizzy sat forward looking out the window. "What a fine stallion he will become."

"Oh, yes, yes." She leaned over Uncle to glimpse the foal. "He is just as you described, Lizzy. Oh, indeed, Phoebe looks quite proud, doesn't she?"

Uncle Henry hemmed. "Phoebe is a very good broodmare—she has certainly paid her way handsomely."

"I only wish I could do the same, sir," said Lavenia.

He sputtered. "There now, Niece, I shall not hear of such talk. A stroke of bad luck hits us all now and again."

Picking at her soiled glove, she nodded. "I hope someday to repay you, Uncle, for your generosity."

"No brooding in my household now. No moping about, weepy and forlorn. A happy face is what I want to behold at the breakfast table." Poking Lizzy with his cane, he quipped, "Even scratches are more welcomed than tears. There now, have I made myself clear, ladies?"

Emily nodded. "Indeed, Uncle."

Lavenia nodded. "Uncle Henry."

Lizzy screwed up her face. "But I simply must cry now and again, sir. If I don't, Uncle Henry, I shall explode into zillions of dreadful pieces."

"Very well, Lizzy, you may explode now and again."

Emily's face puckered, almost to laugh, but held it quite nicely.

"Here we are then, beautiful Neatham Park." Lavenia inhaled deeply and smiled broadly. "Nothing has changed, I see."

"Not in a hundred years," added Uncle, "nor a hundred more, I expect."

As they arrived, the butler, Mr Maxwell, stood under the carriage-porch to receive them. "Good evening, sir."

"Good evening, Mr Maxwell."

"Everything is in good order, sir."

"Hmm, indeed, just as I left it, Mr Maxwell. Mrs Haworth will be staying, indefinitely."

Sniffing the air, he nodded. "Yes, sir."

Uncle took Lavenia's arm. "Supper at eight, as usual." He kissed her forehead. "Do lie down and rest, my dear."

Emily tugged Uncle's sleeve. "And a nap for you, as well, sir."

* * *

The next morning, as the sun shone bright and warm, Lizzy set out for Tillyard Lodge anxious to see if Holly's collar was removed, and, of course, another opportunity to see Sir Edward. Cutting through an apple orchard, winged prey were busy about the fallen fruit—gnats hovered about the bees, the bees mingled about the wasps, the squawky puff-bellied blackbirds flapped about it all—and one in particular, as if wearing a monocle and show-offish, strutted about, his beak bully sharp.

"Now, now, we'll have none of that. You must learn to share," she scolded.

At her tone, the birds scattered high in the trees, and once perched again, peered down at her; the gnats resumed their hovering; the bees returned to their busy work, and Lizzy continued her trek through the hayfield. "Two more fields, two more fences." She trudged on eagerly anticipating seeing the handsome doctor.

Dabbing her brow, she ran her fingers over the tiny lines still healing on her nose, cheek and chin. Glancing at the back of her hands, she shook her head thinking how ugly she must look. Now on the hill overlooking Tillyard Lodge, she heard the sound of hammers and spied some workers busy about the stables.

She frowned. "But, that was Lady Marlboro's special riding area, what could they be doing to it?"

She moved effortlessly down the bridal path and found that the birds who normally gathered at the fountain were now perched in the nearby trees, squawking. The hammering was most annoying to them, she supposed. Stopping to dip her hands into the spurt and splash of the arcing water fountain, she glanced up at an approaching workman. "What is it there you are building?" She pointed to Lady Marlboro's riding arena.

"A special pen for an important horse, I have been told."

"Oh," Lizzy patted her face with the cool drippy water, "an important horse?"

"Miss Bingham wants a colt from Neatham Park brought here."

"What? But it is far too soon to take the foal from Phoebe's side."

He shrugged. "Yes, that's the name Miss Bingham kept repeating: Phoebe," he nodded. "Indeed, miss, the broodmare was called Phoebe. We're to lead her and the foal to that pen," he pointed, "when we are finished."

Lizzy glanced down into the fountain. *But Uncle did not tell me.*

Standing at the front door, Lizzy pulled on the old roaring-lion brass knocker several times. She noticed its teeth long and jagged. *Rather puts me in mind of a certain woman.* Suddenly the door opened.

Johnson looked down his prominent nose. "Miss Doddridge."

"I have come to speak with Sir Edward, Mr Johnson—to see how the pup is coming along."

"Hmm, indeed," he held the door open, "have a seat, Miss Doddridge." Walking a few steps, he stopped and turned back. "I may be a while, miss. Do be patient."

"But of course." Lizzy's brows knit. *When have I ever not been?*

Johnson read her mind, shook his head and resumed in the direction of the magnificent glass conservatory.

Lizzy took a seat, ever mindful for whimpers or barks should Holly be in any great pain. *Would her entire head be bandaged? Would she be able to sniff me out?* She walked to an oil portrait hanging just off the vestibule. *Hmm, a new portrait, I wonder where the Rembrandt is hanging?* She glanced about the room—all the vases were void of flowers. Speaking aloud, she smiled in fond remembrance: "This was Lady Marlboro's sitting room." Casually walking about, she noticed all of her prized knick-knacks were gone. "Well, things have certainly changed, and I dare say not for ..."

"I am glad you find it so, Miss Doddridge." Miss Bingham poked her head around Lady Marlboro's favourite reading chair.

Lizzy stopped, not wanting to look startled, she held her chin quite high, after all, this great house was more hers than Miss Bingham's. She knew its secrets, its history, knew where Jingles, Lady Marlboro's cat, was buried. And she made a mental note to inform Johnson so that no one would dig her up by mistake. She shuddered. *Cat bones ... I should wonder what they look like after five years?*

"Do come in, Miss Doddridge." Miss Bingham stood and carelessly tossed aside *Nicolas Nickleby*.

It was one of Lizzy's favourite books.

And, as if reading Lizzy, like its first chapter, Miss Bingham raised a brow. "So, you like Dickens, do you?"

Startled at such astute observations, Lizzy tried to keep her features in check. "Oh, yes. I admire the author very much." Feeling very smart, she added with such an air, "I have met him, once. Oh, yes, Mores Town End Bookshop, to be exact."

"Really?" She sighed. "He will be coming to stay with us next week—a personal friend of mine, and now Edward's."

Lizzy nodded. "How very nice." *I shall despise Dickens for the rest of my life.* Rubbing her arms briskly, she yawned.

"Yes, I have been very busy redecorating this shabby old place." Walking to the window, she pulled the drapes aside and gazed out. "My wedding present to Edward is tearing down that ghastly glass ... glass house or whatever he calls it." She exhaled in disgust. "I shall have a proper water garden put in."

At such a revelation Lizzy felt dizzy and groped for a chair. "Well, what a surprise that shall be, Miss Bingham." Lizzy felt her gaze spread over her like a spider enfolding a fly. In revulsion, Lizzy shook her head. *God in heaven, surely she would not tear down such a beautiful, wondrous place ...*

"Dear me, Miss Doddridge," she smirked, "you do look a little peaked. Is something wrong? A glass of water perhaps?"

Lizzy rubbed her stomach and swallowed hard. "Thank you, no. I am waiting for Sir Edward, Miss Bingham. I really should be ..."

"There you are, Miss Doddridge." Johnson stood in the doorway. "Right this way."

Lizzy half-curtsied. "Thank you for the water, but I am very well, thank you, Miss Bingham."

"Oh, I am not quite sure of that, Miss Doddridge." Glancing at the butler, she added, "Mr Johnson, do you not think Miss Doddridge looks unwell?"

Quitting the room, Lizzy whispered in a huff, "And you, Miss Bingham, resemble a cartful of cat bones."

Johnson glanced out the window at the gardener as he dug about the garden. "Speaking of cat bones ..."

* * *

"Come in, come in, Miss Elizabeth." Sir Edward's face broke out into a handsome, warm smile. He gestured toward the chair. "Before I take you to see Holly, perhaps you would care for tea?"

Her heart fluttered at his voice. Her face felt flushed, her body heated. "Oh, yes, a cool glass of tea would be wonderful, sir."

Johnson nodded.

"Bring two, Mr Johnson."

Sir Edward came from around his desk, eagerly clasping his hands. "I could not believe my luck when at our engagement ball, but who should accompany Miss Bingham's father, but an old acquaintance of mine."

Lizzy's heart sank when she heard the words 'our engagement ball,' but she smiled and tried hard to concentrate on his words. She likened his voice to the softness of a summer breeze and caught herself gazing at his lips. His teeth were wonderfully white, shaped quite perfectly. She decided he was clearly the most handsome man she had ever ... .

"Miss Elizabeth?"

She read her name on his lips. *Miss Elizabeth?* She glanced up to his eyes, blinking repeatedly. "Me, sir?"

"Yes, you." Walking to the empty, blackened hearth, he turned. "What were you thinking just now, Miss Elizabeth?"

"I was thinking about you, sir." Blushing, she gently ran her fingers over the thin lines yet on her face. "She is going to tear down your magnificent glass house, sir."

Johnson entered the room. Bowing, he lowered the tray to Lizzy.

Lifting her glass, she smiled. "Thank you, Mr Johnson."

Sir Edward took his. "That will be all, Johnson."

"Very well, sir."

They watched as he quietly left the room.

"Miss Elizabeth, do not let Miss Bingham concern you. I shall overcome whatever she chooses to do."

Lizzy would have nothing of it. "I have heard quite enough, sir. Please, Sir Edward, tell me about Holly—she has survived?"

He drew back. "Survived? Miss Elizabeth, while you were studying my physiognomy just moments ago, I was trying to explain that an acquaintance, Professor Meir from the Royal Veterinary College, kindly consented to remove Holly's collar— an old rope, so it was. I was honoured to assist him in the surgery."

"Oh, indeed, Sir Edward. What good news that is."

"Indeed, and the pup is doing marvellously well. Within the week she will be running and playing amongst the best of dogs."

For the first time that evening, Lizzy's face brightened. "Oh, sir, how wonderful for her. Your acquaintance, Professor Meir, must be a very considerate gentleman."

"You may express your feelings to him personally. Come now." Stepping aside, he opened a door and gestured for her to enter.

Walking into the room, Lizzy stopped and sniffed the air. "Very much like a hospital, sir." She rubbed her nose. There was a strong odour of something, but she could not put a name to it—perhaps sulphur.

"Well, this is my office. I suppose it smells very much like a hospital in some ways—I do my research here when not in London." Opening another door, he motioned for her to enter. "This way, Miss Elizabeth, I shall introduce you to my friend."

Following alongside Sir Edward down a long, dimly lit and narrow hallway, Lizzy took in his most excellent scent. "Mmm, lavender, sir, how well I love lavender, particularly lavender soap." Inhaling deeply, she sighed. "Oh, indeed, every evening as I slowly sink down into my warm bath water, I lather up my sponge and watch the tiny purple bubbles float across the bow of my ... ." She stopped at an open window. There growing in huge abundance were lavender bushes, in full, glorious bloom.

"Float across the bow of your ... ? Do go on, Miss Elizabeth."

"I thought it was you, Sir Edward. I thought that lovely scent was coming from you."

Stopping, he turned to her and smiled. "How kind of you, Miss Elizabeth, how very kind. I must admit lavender *is* one of my favourites—though I do not bathe in it."

"Then you must do so, Sir Edward."

Lizzy couldn't see the blush envelope his face, but noticed his breathing sharpen.

"Well, well then, here we are." In the tight hallway, he had to lean into her to open the door.

She stopped breathing; her lips parted, she felt his warm, sweet breath, "Oh, God in heaven," she whispered and closed her eyes, "yes, please do."

"Miss Elizabeth," he gently pushed the door open, "here we are then."

Professor Meir glanced up. "Oh, there you are Sir Edward, I was ... ."

Lizzy's chin was still tilted up, her eyes closed, her lips partly open. Both men stared at her.

Sir Edward's face turned crimson. "Miss Elizabeth," he repeated.

She opened her eyes.

"Professor Meir, allow me the honour of introducing Miss Elizabeth Doddridge, Neatham Park, my neighbour just a hill and vale away."

Meir watched her in bewildered amusement.

Lizzy lowered her chin, blinked several times and held out her hand, smiling. "Professor Meir, I am very grateful you love animals, sir." Her eyes glistened. "I do too."

A smile broke out on his face. He took her hand and kissed it. "I can see that, Miss Doddridge."

As if sensing the bond that had immediately formed between the two, Sir Edward moved swiftly to her side. "Indeed," he took her elbow, "Holly will be very excited to see you, Miss Elizabeth."

Lizzy glanced up at him, her eyes sparkling. "I very much want to see her, sir."

Clearly taken with the lovely Miss Doddridge, Professor Meir bowed. "Then come this way." He took Lizzy's other elbow, smiling. "Come, come."

Sir Edward was forced to follow close at Lizzy's free side, and was forced to hear the account of the surgery—Professor Meir's explanation of how he did this and how he did that. How well the dog behaved, how long Holly was under the anaesthesia, what an excellent patient and so on and so forth.

"Indeed," interjected Sir Edward at every opportunity, but at every turn he was ignored.

Lizzy seemed mesmerised by the professor's detail and commented frequently as she kissed and fondled the squirming Holly. "Oh, sir, how wonderful a surgeon you are."

Watching the two, Sir Edward stood back, looking glum. Glancing now and again at Lizzy, then at the professor, crossing his arms, he hemmed; hemmed louder until finally, she looked up.

"Sir Edward, do you want me?"

"Perhaps a word."

Professor Meir, Lizzy, and Holly stared at him.

Lizzy nodded. "Indeed, sir, do go on."

"In private, Miss Elizabeth."

"Oh, but of course, sir."

Sir Edward nodded politely. "Excuse us, Professor Meir, I shall be just a moment."

Escorting Lizzy back out into the hallway, he pulled the door closed. "Miss Elizabeth," he whispered, "I must inform you that Professor Meir has ten children."

Her eyes widened. "Ten?"

He glanced at the ceiling. "I thought you should know."

Though the hallway was dim, she could see that one peculiar vein on his neck that would swell when he became provoked. She touched it gently. "That vein in your neck, Sir Edward. It is swollen and pulsing again. Have I done something to upset you?"

"You are more than observant, Miss Elizabeth. No, you have not done anything to upset me. It is just that Professor Meir's wife died just last year and … ."

She studied his lovely mouth. "And?"

"Well, he has a daughter your age."

* * *

Entering through the kitchen of Neatham Park, Lizzy removed her muddy boots. Now in her bare stockings, she walked through the dining room and into the hall. "Hello," she called. "Hello," she called again. Turning to ascend the stairs she heard someone crying. Listening carefully, she decided it was coming from the drawing room. Opening the door quietly, she spied Emily holding Lavenia's hand.

"Emily, what is wrong?"

Exhaling deeply, she pressed Lavenia's hand. "I just told her of Abby's demise."

Lizzy knelt by her side. "I know the pain, dear." She wept with her. "Abby was a wonderful dog."

Lavenia nodded through her tears, dabbing her nose. "I heard how wonderful you were to her—how you slept next to her on the floor all night. I shall never forget your kindness, Elizabeth, never." She kissed the top of her head. "You are a saint." Turning to Emily, she kissed her too. "I will lie down now, please excuse me."

Lizzy stood. "I shall help you to your room, Lavenia."

"No, no, dearest. Please, I am able." Moving slowly to the door, she turned. "I shall have supper in my room."

"Of course, Cousin," Lizzy half-smiled, "we understand."

They watched as Lavenia quitted the room.

"I did not hear you come in, Lizzy." Glancing down, she frowned. "You are in your stocking feet?"

"My boots were muddy, Em. I left them to be cleaned."

"You walked back from Tillyard Lodge in this weather?"

"Oh, no, an acquaintance of Sir Edward's, Professor Meir, a veterinary surgeon was leaving for London, and he kindly offered to bring me home."

"A veterinarian, Lizzy?"

"He and Sir Edward operated on Holly, quite successfully, all in all." She sighed. "You should see how wonderful Holly looks, Em. Why, within the week she will be running and playing like a normal dog."

"That is very good news. Now, tell about this veterinarian, Lizzy."

"Well, he is quite handsome, professes at The Royal Veterinary College, has ten children, a daughter my age, and his wife died several years ago."

"Ten children?" Emily shook her head. "There is no wonder how she died."

The study door opened, and Uncle Henry shuffled in. Turning, he poked the door with his cane closing it rather abruptly. "Now then, who died?"

The door suddenly reopened and Mr Maxwell, rubbing his nose, entered. "Beg pardon, sir, but dinner is served."

"Again," said Uncle, "Who died?"

"The wife of someone we do not know, a Professor Meir from London, a veterinary surgeon," said Emily.

"Indeed, Uncle," Lizzy nodded, "he is an acquaintance of Sir Edward."

"Oh, right, regarding the pup." Entering the dining room, Uncle sniffed the air. "Aah, turtle soup. So, how is the pup coming along, Lizzy?"

"Sir Edward requested that I come every day to walk the dog." She took her seat. "He is much too busy to walk her. He feels Holly will heal faster if she has exercise and loving attention."

He nodded. "Indeed."

"And what of the professor, Lizzy?" Emily sat down snapping open her napkin.

"He is to return to Tillyard Lodge next week—to see Holly again. He wants to make sure she is healing properly."

"All the way from London?" said Emily. "I should say the surgeon is very conscientious."

"They are building a new stall in Lady Marlboro's riding arena, Em."

"Oh, dear me," Emily frowned, "her ladyship would not like that, I'm afraid."

"Indeed, what a bad stroke of luck for her, then." Uncle Henry dabbed his lips with his napkin.

"A bad stroke of luck, sir?"

"That she died and wouldn't have to witness such a travesty."

"Uncle Henry," said Lizzy dipping into her soup, "I was told by one of the workmen at Tillyard that when the stall is completed, they will bring Phoebe and the colt there. Can that be so?"

"Phoebe will be leaving us, sir? Why, we have never let her out of our sight before," said Emily setting down her spoon.

"Do not be alarmed, my dear. She will stay there only until the foal is weaned, Dr North suggested it."

"Yes, yes, I remember Sir Edward declaring the colt was bred for Miss Bingham. Indeed, I believe she has been pushing

Sir Edward all along. I have come to dislike the lady immensely," said Lizzy.

Emily drew back. "Mind your manners, girl."

"Now, now, Lizzy, that is not it at all. Dr North worried that when it came time to wean the colt, Phoebe would be prancing, whinnying, and stomping about days on end. You know how she gets when they take her babies away. He was concerned about *you*, Lizzy," said Uncle.

"Well then, it is obvious he realises how tender-hearted you are, dear." Emily patted her hand. "Sister, he must think very highly of you."

Lizzy blushed, feeling her heart swell. "Forgive me Uncle, it is just that ... ."

"Nothing to forgive Lizzy, you had no idea, Sir Edward was so thoughtful. Not many real gentlemen around anymore."

Emily set down her cup to the saucer. "So, Lizzy, tell me about the inside of the house. I hear Miss Bingham is changing everything."

"Indeed she is, Em, but she won't be able to change *him*."

Uncle glanced up. "Him?"

Chapter 5 – A Wedding at St Paul's Cathedral

It was a brisk, orange October afternoon as Lizzy stood shivering at the window. Tightening her wool scarf about her neck, she watched the leaden sky, thinking that such a sky often brought thick troublesome clouds. And this afternoon was no exception—there in Uncle Henry's mail salver sat the wedding-invitation-troublesome-cloud.

"Well, what else could it be, Em? Of course, it is Sir Edward's wedding invitation." In a huff, Lizzy walked across the room and stood over the letter. Finally picking it up, she sniffed the envelope, juggled it, and held it up to the window light.

Emily scolded, "Dearest, please, put it down this instant."

Squinting through the fine paper envelope, Lizzy huffed, "Hmm, here we are then, St. Paul's Cathedral, 1 p.m., 1 December." She frowned. "I cannot make out more, Em."

"St. Paul's?" Lavenia straightened. "Oh, if only I were not so fat with child. How I would love to attend—no doubt a few royals will be there."

"I should not like to be there, I assure you." Lizzy fanned herself with the letter.

"They must be inviting a considerable crowd to be using the Cathedral," said Emily.

"No doubt the Queen will be there," said Lizzy.

"December?" Lavenia quivered. "I think not. December is too cold, blustery. Could snow at a moment's notice."

Still gazing at the unopened invitation, Lizzy fretted. "Where has Uncle Henry gone off to that he did not open his mail?"

"He will be here shortly, Lizzy. Calm yourself." Emily set aside her knitting. "You had better put that letter back or ... ."

The door creaked opened.

Lizzy quickly hid the letter behind her back.

Uncle Henry entered. "Good afternoon, ladies." Spying Lizzy at the hearth, he smiled. "Dearest, do be a darling and bring the letter to me." Squirming in next to Lavenia, he affectionately patted her hand. "You are looking well, my dear."

"Thank you, Uncle. I assure you, sir, I feel quite uncomfortable, but I shall try very hard not be a bore."

"Here you are, Uncle Henry." Lizzy handed him the letter.

He nodded. "Helen informs me that Dr North and his bride will be travelling to Paris, Brussels, Rome—a honeymoon as well as medical conventions. They should be gone a very long time."

Lizzy removed to the window and stood, arms folded, staring at nothing.

Uncle tore open the letter. "St. Paul's Cathedral, 1 p.m., 1 December. Hmm, dear me, December." He rubbed his eyes. "Cold." He glanced at Lizzy. "We are all invited, but are we *all* going?"

"Well, I suppose we should, Uncle Henry," said Emily.

"Elizabeth?"

"Yes, sir, I shall go ... if you wish it."

"Though I cannot go, sir," lamented Lavenia, "I would so love to ogle over the latest fashions, hear the most recent gossip." She sighed. "It is a pity that I am so removed from city life." Glancing at Uncle, she quickly corrected, "Oh, but sir, I cannot tell you how happy I am here."

"There, there," Uncle Henry took her hand, "you mustn't cry Lavenia darling. We are all here to help you."

"I cannot imagine how utterly ruthless Rupert has behaved, Uncle Henry. Why, just this morning I overheard one of the servants say how he poisoned Abby and all her pups."

"Except one," said Lizzy.

"Lavenia, all that is behind us now," said Uncle.

"The servants were talking about Holly—the pup you found, Lizzy. Had I known what a scoundrel Rupert was, I would have never married him, I assure you." Trying to find a comfortable position, she moaned, "I hope as long as I live, I shall never see that devil man again."

"We all hope to never see the man again, Lavenia, but perhaps someday he will want to see his child," said Uncle.

"I shall forbid such a visit, sir. I plan on divorcing him soon after the child is born."

Lizzy nodded in agreement. "Indeed, what sort of man would kill innocent animals?"

Frowning at her, Emily held a finger to her lips.

Lizzy hemmed. "Excuse me, Cousin."

Mr Maxwell entered. "Sir, there is a gentleman calling, a Professor Meir." He handed him his card.

Lizzy jumped up, smiling. "Oh, dear me, yes, Professor Meir, Uncle, he operated on Holly. Do see him in, Maxwell."

After Emily helped Lavenia slip on her shoes, she quickly slicked back her hair, gathered herself up, and sat attentively.

Professor Meir entered the room. With an air of accomplished confidence, he scanned their faces. "Miss Elizabeth." He smiled and took her hand.

"Oh, Professor Meir," Lizzy curtsied slightly, "how good of you to come, sir."

He nodded. "Thank you. I have been meaning to call ... ." he glanced at Emily. As if he had met her somewhere before, he held her gaze. His face softened.

"Sir," Lizzy interrupted the pause, "allow me to introduce my family. This is my dearest Uncle Doddridge, my cousin, Mrs Rupert Haworth, and my sister, Miss Emily Doddridge."

He slowly took Emily's hand, holding her gaze, he kissed her hand. His shiny face grew pink. "We have met before?"

She purred, "Yes, somewhere."

Lizzy was a little taken aback at her sister's demeanour. *Somewhere?*

Uncle Henry nodded. "Elizabeth has told us what an excellent surgeon you are, sir. We marvel at your conscientiousness to a lowly dog and commend you, Professor."

Lavenia moaned and sat back. Dabbing her lips with her handkerchief, she looked peaked.

The professor moved to her side. "Oh, dear me, madam, are you unwell?"

Emily knelt by Lavenia's side. "Discussing injured animals unnerves our cousin, sir."

Straightening, the professor nodded, looking perplexed. "Indeed, then," he hemmed, "we shall refrain."

Lizzy put her arm around Lavenia. "Professor, our cousin, Mrs Haworth, is most recently from London."

"Oh, indeed. I also have a townhouse there, in Coinandpenny."

Lavenia nodded. "Ah, yes, but a little distance from our townhouse. She set down her teacup and smiled at Lizzy. "Be a dear and help me up, will you?"

"Your home is very near the hospital, is it not, Professor?" said Lavenia making polite conversation as she stood.

"Yes, very near it," he replied glancing once more to Emily.

Masking her discomfort, Lavenia took Lizzy's hand. "Professor, please excuse me, will you, sir? I must rest."

Lizzy nodded. "Please, sir, excuse me as well. I will see Mrs Haworth to her room. I shall return shortly."

"Certainly, I do understand," he said with a half-bow, "good day now."

"Professor Meir," said Emily, very happy to be wearing her most flattering supper gown, "a glass of sherry perhaps?"

* * *

Within the hour Lizzy returned to the drawing room to find Emily and Professor Meir sitting together on the small red velvet settee, Uncle had drifted off to sleep.

Meir stood. "I was explaining to your lovely sister, Miss Doddridge that I have been away to Brussels at a veterinary convention."

"Oh, indeed, sir," said Lizzy taking a seat nearest the fire. Uncle Henry sputtered but remained asleep. She was eager to hear Professor Meir and anything that had to do with animals—how many he had saved, his new techniques, new medicines.

"And Professor Meir," Emily glowed, "how did you find Brussels?"

The conversation between the blushing Emily and the obliging professor went on uninterrupted for what seemed like hours. Lizzy leaned back smiling to herself. Watching the mantle clock as it struck eleven and then twelve, and not once did the two hear the chimes. *Perhaps they hear their own.*

Lizzy stood and rubbed her arms briskly. Staring into the dying embers, she moaned to herself. "I do believe the room is too chilly."

Meir and Emily's gazes never left one another as they continued on with their conversation.

Lizzy shrugged. "Well, I am still a little chilly, if you two are not."

And still they continued on as if she were not there.

Lizzy tugged on the rope pull and even as Helen re-stoked the fire, adding three logs, did the professor momentarily glance her way, but only to be enthralled with Emily's most fervent opinion on Lord Byron's poem of man's last days on earth.

Helen curtsied. "Will that be all, Miss Lizzy?"

"Professor Meir will be staying for lunch, Helen."

Helen glanced at the two and smiled. "Yes, ma'am."

* * *

Standing on the carriage-porch, Emily waved goodbye to Professor Meir. Snuggling into her hooded cape, she watched his horses prance through the late afternoon rain. The Neatham Park road is long and narrow as it weaves its way through the small village of Bentley.

If one cared to watch a carriage travel that little bit of road as it left the village where it opened onto the London Road, they could stand on a wee stone ledge very near the porch. Emily stood on that ledge and watched Meir's carriage pass over the Wey River disappearing into the thick, dark forest.

Opening the door, Lizzy glanced out at the darkening sky. "Emily, dearest, shall I light the torch?"

Patting her heart, she smiled wistfully. "It is lit. Now, help me down, will you?"

Feeling the crisp early evening air, Lizzy shivered and took her sister's hand. "Dear me, your fingers are like ice. Come, warm your hands at the fire before you take a chill."

Just before entering the house, Emily glanced back over her shoulder.

Lizzy giggled. "Love, is it?"

She nodded with a smile. "Wilhelm will call on me next week—he is to visit with Dr North for a few days."

"Wilhelm? Hmm, well now, the professor certainly made short work of lengthy introductions, protocol, etcetera."

As Emily dreamily brushed by her, she sighed. "Etcetera, indeed. We certainly did do away with the formalities of the early acquaintance gibberish." Giggling she reached out and tweaked Lizzy's nose.

"Stop, Em. It will grow long if you do not stop pulling it. Humph, Wilhelm, indeed, is German." She rubbed her nose. "Well, Prince Albert is German. If a German is good enough for the Queen ... ."

"Really, Lizzy, Wilhelm was born here. He is an Englishman through and through."

"How intriguing all of this is becoming, Emily." Smiling, she entered the drawing room and stood at the hearth.

"Intriguing? Why do you say intriguing?" Emily tossed her wrap to Helen.

Lizzy shrugged. "Well, it is just that Professor Meir is a good friend of Sir Edward's, and I simply find it intriguing that we are becoming a more integral part of Sir Edward's society."

Emily's brow arched. "Forgive the sour note, Lizzy, but we are also becoming an integral part of Miss Bingham's as well."

"I shall never become an integral part of *her* society, I assure you, Emily." She anxiously wrung her hands over the fire. "Indeed, the very idea."

"Of course not, dearest, how silly of me to even consider such a thought."

* * *

The following week a courier arrived at Neatham Park. Helen found Uncle resting in the sunroom.

"Beg pardon, sir, a letter by courier. Dr North, London."

Uncle sat up and glanced at the envelope. Adjusting his spectacles, he began reading aloud:

"1 November – London
Dear Mr Doddridge,
Sir, forgive the written word, but I have been
terribly busy with my research. I had planned on visiting
Tillyard Lodge one last time before the wedding, but
Miss Bingham has informed me of the impossibility. I
had wished to have Phoebe and the colt moved to their
new home before the weather turns. Therefore, I would
wish it to be done very soon. I await your approval, Mr
Doddridge, before I send my grooms. We have discussed

the reasons before, tender hearts, etc. etc. One last thing
Sir, I place myself at your humble mercy and desire that
your most kind niece, Miss Elizabeth Doddridge, look
after Holly while I am away on honeymoon. I would be
most grateful Sir.
　　　Yours very truly,
　　　Dr Edward North

There now, Lizzy," said Uncle, "Dr North thinks highly of
you. He has singled you out to care for Holly." He handed the
letter to her.

Taking it, she smiled. "Indeed, Uncle."

"Very well then, Lizzy, I shall write the good doctor and
inform him that his wishes will be taken care of."

7 November – Neatham Park
Dear Dr North,
　　　Sir, I have already taken the liberty of having
Phoebe and the colt delivered to Tillyard Lodge. Fine
prospect the two shall have there. Oh, yes, Miss
Doddridge and Miss Elizabeth wept at the news of
Phoebe and her colt leaving Neatham Park ... Lizzy
insisted upon riding Phoebe to Tillyard herself—she was
more than happy to honour your request that she look in
on Holly while you are gone. I assure you, sir, on that
aspect, she was more than pleased—she adores that dog.
　　　I look forward to having the opportunity of seeing
you in London, sir, at your wedding. Best wishes.
　　　H. H. Doddridge

* * *

Anxious to look after Holly, Lizzy set out early to Tillyard
Lodge. Now standing at its door, she noticed a new ring-bell
had been installed. "Humph, another modern change." She
used the gnarly brass lion-headed knocker to announce her
coming instead, clanging it several times.

The roaring lion-head knocker had been there for well
over a hundred years, she suspected, but Miss Bingham, no

doubt, had it replaced with a *proper bell*. Clanging the knocker again with impatience, Lizzy startled when Johnson suddenly opened the door. Glancing at the bell-pull, he sighed wearily, "We do have an outside ringer now, you know, Miss Elizabeth."

"Oh, yes, so I have noticed." She invited herself in. "I have come to entertain Holly, Mr Johnson." She rubbed her arms. "Oh, it is much colder in here than outside." She glanced around. "There is no fire?"

"No, Miss Doddridge, there is no fire."

Lizzy had heard gossip from Mary and Helen that Miss Bingham wished strict economy at Tillyard. She had left word that during daylight *all* rooms were to be without fires.

"So," Lizzy shook her head, "it is true what I heard. I do hope the servants' quarters have heat."

Johnson frowned. "Good news travels fast."

"Nothing escapes Mary and Helen, Mr Johnson."

He glanced down. "Miss Elizabeth, Sir Edward did leave word that you would be tending the dog, but ..."

She looked up into his sad, grey eyes. "But what Mr Johnson?" She sensed a wrongdoing. "Has something happened to Holly?"

"Miss Bingham took her, Miss Doddridge."

"To London?"

Pursing his lips, he nodded. "I advised her of Sir Edward's wishes—showed her your Uncle's letter stating that you would look after the dog, but she promptly tossed it into the fire, miss. I am truly sorry."

"God in heaven," she whispered, "she is more wicked than I had ever dared to imagine." She glanced about the dark, dank room. "Very well then, Mr Johnson, I shall go."

"Beg pardon, Miss Elizabeth," his face drew pale, "but I am afraid Sir Edward's conservatory is to be torn down soon."

"Yes, I know. How unfortunate. It is to be a wedding present ... *she* will replace it with who knows what sort of monstrosity."

He cleared his throat. "Unfortunate, indeed."

"Mr Johnson, what will they do with the old glass?"

"Break it and bury it, I would suppose. Miss Bingham wants it done away with."

"I see." Glancing about the room, she sighed. "Lady Marlboro had a fire in every room, Mr Johnson."

Holding the door, he bowed. "So I have been told."

"Who is removing the conservatory?"

"The Millers, from Alton."

"Thank you, Mr Johnson." She climbed into her one-horse gig. "Mr Johnson, I will look in on Phoebe and the colt before I leave ... unless, of course, she has taken them too."

"No, Miss, she had not the room." He closed the door silently.

* * *

Back at Neatham, Lizzy threw off her cape and stormed into the study where she found Uncle, Emily, and Lavenia.

"Alton?" Emily glanced questioningly at Lizzy. "I know of no one in Alton."

"Well, I wish to speak with the Millers there and very soon."

"Do we know any Millers? I think not, dearest," said Lavenia.

Uncle Henry set down his book. "I believe the Miller tribe lives near the old grind mill."

"They are to tear down Sir Edward's conservatory, Uncle. Miss Bingham has ordered its removal. I must recover the pieces ... save them. What will Sir Edward think when he returns to find his sanctuary gone?" Fretting, she took a seat and folded her arms in disgust. "The very idea."

With a stern look, Uncle straightened. "Lizzy, you must not meddle in their affairs."

"But Uncle, if I retrieve the glass and store it here, what is the harm?"

Emily shook her head. "Lizzy, Uncle is right. You must not pry. And, why, dearest, do you wish to bring the glass here?"

"Someday he may wish to have it restored."

Lavenia sat up. "Lizzy is right. What harm is there in taking the glass and storing it? Who is to care one way or the other? It would be such a shame to destroy lovely conservatory glass. Oh, I once had such a room when I was a little girl." She sighed at the recollection. "Aunt Lucille would take me on strolls through it. The lovely flowers were magnificent."

Uncle Henry softened. "Yes, yes, my dearest Lucille. Indeed," his eyes welled with tears, "my dearest Lucille, how she loved her flowers." He looked at Lizzy. "Well, I suppose there is no harm, but I would wish it of you, Lizzy, not to say a word that you have it brought here. I would not like to cause any trouble."

"I promise you, Uncle, I shall not say a word." Lizzy's face turned a deep pink. "Sir, one more thing, I must share with you, Miss Bingham took Holly with her to London."

Uncle took in a deep, frowning breath. "Pity, pity all of it. You were so fond of the little creature."

Lavenia patted Lizzy's hand. "I shall despise Miss Bingham for the rest of my life, Elizabeth. Depend upon it."

"Thank you, dearest Lavenia." Lizzy lifted her quivering chin. "Together we shall despise her all our lives."

"Dear me, you will only succeed in spoiling your good thoughts if you harbour ill will against anyone," said Emily.

"Indeed, my dear young ladies, 'Self-righteousness is the devil's masterpiece to make us think well of ourselves.' " [4]

"Forgive me, Uncle," said Lizzy. "That was most unkind." She exchanged glances with Lavenia.

[4] Thomas Adams (1583-1652) English clergyman. Quoted from *A Dictionary of Thoughts* by Tryon Edwards (1908).

Chapter 6 – Death Hath No Favourites

St. Paul's Cathedral appeared to their left as the Doddridge carriage pulled up behind the others. London's finest society moved briskly along the pavement toward the church. It was the wedding of the year, the wealthy Bingham family's daughter, Miss Beatrice Bingham and Dr Edward North, were to wed within the hour.

The air was heavy with spits of thick rain; shiny black umbrellas bobbled throughout the crowd.

Entering the dark, bone-chilling wedding place, Lizzy walked slowly behind Emily and Uncle Doddridge. They were eventually ushered into an old pew of shiny dark oak.

"To the end, sir," directed the young, sober-faced usher, "the very end."

"I should need a spyglass, Em. I cannot see one thing." Lizzy shook her head. "Not that I shall miss anything."

"Yes," Uncle Henry squirmed on the hard oak plank, peeking around the multitude of ladies' hats that blocked his view, "we are a far distance away."

Emily straightened. "I can see Dr North." Squinting, she added, "My, but he is wearing a most serious face, Lizzy."

"Is it the *I am going to vomit any second* face, Emily?"

A lady, wearing an oversized black-feathered hat, sitting directly in front of her, glanced back and frowned.

Lizzy smiled. "Or ... is it the, I really must be going face?"

In a huff, the lady whispered to her husband, "What a nerve, Horace."

The organ began. The boys' choir began. The huge white sanctuary candles sputtered and licked at the cold December air as it swirled about the Cathedral. Lizzy likened it to an ill wind.

"I cannot hear a word they are saying," Emily lamented, "not a word."

"Why, it is a blessing, then." Lizzy shivered under her wrap. She noticed a loose thread dangling from the huffy lady's black hat.

Emily shook her head. "No."

*　*　*

Leaving the Cathedral, Lizzy squinted up into the late afternoon drizzle. "How nice to have seen Sir Roger and Lady Mary, Emily."

"Yes," she cupped her hand to her mouth, whispering, "I couldn't help but notice she is with child."

"I was sworn to secrecy, Em," she glanced around. "I have been invited to stay with her for a few weeks after the baby is born." Lizzy opened her umbrella and shielded Uncle Henry from the rain. Inhaling deeply, she smiled. "I think I shall like doing that very much."

Emily hugged her. "And how are *you* doing, Lizzy?"

She lifted her chin bravely. "I shall survive, Em. Though I am very thankful I did not hear Sir Edward's voice—hear his vows to her."

"Yes, I noticed you stuck your fingers in your ears."

Sighing, Lizzy bit her lip. "I simply could not bear the words, Emily."

Arriving at the waiting carriage, Uncle Henry stopped and fondly gazed into Lizzy's teary eyes. Kissing her cheek, he smiled. "I admire you Elizabeth, always true to your convictions. 'One life; a little gleam of time between two eternities; no second chance for us forever more.' "[5]   He pressed her gloved hand. "Patience, my dear—your love will come, Lizzy."

"Mr Doddridge, so good to see you again, sir," said Professor Meir as he came up behind them.

Emily's face gladdened. Turning to the voice, she smiled.

Uncle Henry extended his hand. "Good afternoon, Professor Meir."

---

[5] Thomas Carlyle (1795-1881) Scottish philosopher. Quoted from *A Dictionary of Thoughts* by Tryon Edwards (1908).

Removing his hat, the professor nodded to Lizzy and smiled warmly at Emily, his face now rather flush. "Did you find the wedding a pleasant experience, Miss Emily?"

"Oh, sir," she nodded, "weddings are always a pleasant experience."

"Yes," he held her gaze, "yes, I have found them so. And you have come from Neatham Park?"

"Yes, we have."

"Why," he said with great kindness, "you must all be exhausted." Glancing at Uncle Doddridge, he gestured, "Sir, you and your nieces must come to my home for a little warmth, a little sherry, perhaps. It is not so very far, you know."

Nodding appreciatively, Uncle Henry smiled with acceptance. "How considerate of you sir, though we have our own townhouse nearby, we would be more than pleased ..." He grabbed his chest, his pale face twisted, his jaw dropped.

"God in heaven, Uncle," cried Lizzy. She tried to steady him, but he folded and dropped to the wet pavement clutching his chest. His black silk hat toppled into the gutter.

Kneeling by his side, Emily held her umbrella over his open, lifeless eyes. "Oh, dear Uncle."

The thick rain had turned to slush; the carriage horses stomped with impatience, passers-by huddled about, whispering, staring, pointing. A policeman respectfully covered the dear old gentleman with his coat. Soon an ambulance wagon arrived, drawn by two calm and obedient black horses, and he was taken away.

"I would be honoured, Miss Emily, if you and your sister would take refuge in my home." Professor Meir took her elbow. "Come now, it is only a little distance."

Emily's face was ashen, her hair soaked, the netting on her hat hung heavy and black with slushy rain. She took his gloved hand. "Thank you, Wilhelm. We would be most grateful."

He removed his hat. "Indeed, my dear."

Lizzy touched his sleeve. "Do ride with us, sir. Our carriage is just there."

As their carriage ambled past St. Paul's Cathedral, the once crowded sidewalk was now barren, black and shiny—silent as glass. It had begun to snow.

* * *

While in the carriage, Professor Meir sat stoic and sombre. Emily and Lizzy kept their heads bowed. Their muffs sitting obediently on their laps, their hands remained still.

The professor hemmed. "Of my ten children, I have two sons yet at home."

Emily looked up. "They did not accompany you, Wilhelm?"

"Stuart is ten, and Charles is twelve, Miss Emily. They do not enjoy weddings, particularly formal ones such as this."

Lizzy bowed her head. "Indeed."

Professor Meir straightened and glanced out. "Well then, here we are, my home." The carriage ambled to a stop.

Two young boys stood at the open door, waving excitedly. "Father," said one, "you must come, be quick, sir!"

Emily and Lizzy followed the professor as he flew up the snow-covered steps and into the house.

"What is it, Charles?" he said, panting, trying to catch his breath.

"Ripper tore up cook's slippers again. She is chasing him about the kitchen with a broom! Hurry Father or she will whack him senseless."

Meir threw off his coat on a waiting chair, shrugged at Emily, and ran down the hall calling back over his shoulder, "Do make yourselves comfortable."

Emily covered her mouth, shaking her head. "Very well."

Lizzy peeked into what she deemed to be the parlour. "Emily, this must be where we are to make ourselves comfortable."

Following her into the warm, cosy room, Emily tugged at her gloves. "What a blessing it was that you met the professor, Lizzy."

"I think he is in love with you, Em, very much in love with you."

"Yes, I know." She fumbled with her gloves. "Strange how one knows such things so soon after meeting."

Standing by the warmth of the hearth fire, Lizzy chaffed her hands and wept. "Oh, what a horrible day this has become."

Emily sighed deeply. "I cannot find the words, poor dear Uncle." She brought her handkerchief to her eyes. "Poor dear Uncle Doddridge."

Suddenly little chirps erupted from one corner of the room.

Lizzy lit up. "Canaries." She rushed to the caged birds. "Look, Em, how lovely they are, but a sweet breath of life on this horrid day."

Professor Meir entered, his sons huddled close behind him. "Forgive my hasty departure, ladies. Good cooks are hard to find." Shaking his head, he apologised, "Our newest puppy is teething."

Lizzy nodded. "Oh, yes, Professor, we understand."

"Charles and Stuart," said the professor to his sons as he moved aside, "do meet Miss Emily Doddridge and her sister, Miss Elizabeth Doddridge."

They, each in turn, took Lizzy and Emily's hand and extended a polite welcome. They then sat down quietly, one gentlemanly and the other, awkwardly.

Lizzy noticed right off the jagged hole in Stuart's shoe—obviously a puppy chew. Dabbing her lips, she glanced away thinking him a dear boy.

The maid bustled in with a lovely silver tea service and deftly arranged the sugars, crème and napkins ... everything quite nicely. Glancing nervously toward the ladies, she curtsied and left.

Lizzy nodded to the professor. "How very thoughtful, Professor Meir."

"Please, Miss Elizabeth, you must call me Wilhelm, as your sister does."

Emily nodded to her with a wee smile.

The maid returned. "Professor, there is a caller." She handed him his calling-card.

Hastily reading it, the professor stood. "Please excuse me, I shall not be long."

Emily and Lizzy resumed their glum countenance.

Stuart and Charles paid particular attention to Emily, looking her up and down with curiosity.

Lifting her chin, Emily apologised, "I do not always look this dishevelled. It has been a trying day."

Charles straightened. "Oh, no, ma'am, you look beautiful." His freckled face reddened.

Watching the youngster, Lizzy smiled, grateful for the kind diversion.

Stuart fidgeted in his seat. "Father warned us to be reserved and quiet. We are sorry for the death of your uncle, Miss Doddridge, and Miss Emily Doddridge." He glanced about the room. "We have three dogs if you would like to see them."

"Three dogs?" said Lizzy looking a little astounded.

"And two cats," Charles added with a proud nod, his cowlick pointing toward the ceiling.

Emily hemmed demurely, "Perhaps later, thank you."

Stuart scooted forward on his chair and whispered to Emily, "Father had to promise the cook a new pair of slippers so that she would not leave again."

She nodded. "Indeed, a very wise decision."

Lizzy smiled at the boys. "Indeed, very good news, one must keep the cook happy."

The professor's sons were pleasant enough lads to be sure, she thought. The house was a busy affair with three dogs, two cats, canaries, bowls of fish sitting about as a vase full of flowers would be.

The professor came back into the room and half-bowed. "Miss Emily and Miss Elizabeth, if you would please excuse my sons?"

"Certainly, Wilhelm." Emily smiled at the boys as they left the room.

Professor Meir returned shortly. He positioned a chair close to Emily and Lizzy. In a low tone, he whispered, "I was just speaking with the mortician." His face saddened. "He managed the affairs of my dearest wife last year—an excellent man, I assure you."

Emily nodded, her voice faltering. "In ... indeed."

"I presumed your uncle is to be buried at Neatham Park?"

"Yes," responded Emily, "next to his wife, Aunt Lucille."

"I see." He paused for a moment. "If you wish it, you may both stay the night here—you are more than welcome."

"Thank you, sir, for your kindness, but we have a townhouse here, and our nanny is there. She must be informed of Uncle Doddridge's death. Nan has been with us since we were born." She glanced at Lizzy. "And, we have our cousin, Mrs Haworth, to consider. She awaits our return this evening at Neatham Park."

Lizzy sighed. "Indeed, Professor, she is with child, and I do not know exactly how she will take the news."

"Oh, dear me, yes, I remember." He clasped his hands in a sorrowful gesture.

"We must consider her feelings and wishes, Wilhelm," said Emily.

"And Nan's," added Lizzy.

He nodded. "But of course." Studying his hands, he continued, "Well, then, considering Mrs Haworth, I would suggest that you leave London soon. I will instruct Mr Flannigan, the mortician, to leave shortly after you." Glancing up, he squinted at the window. "It has quit snowing, the sky is fair. The road looks to be in good condition, and there is good light yet to travel in."

Lizzy lowered her head into her hands and wept. "Thank you, sir. I cannot tell you how grateful my sister and I are for your most excellent guidance and the kindnesses shown to us."

"I assure you, it was the least I could do. I would also wish it that you do not travel without a chaperone. I would be most honoured to see you safely home."

Emily's chin quivered. "Thank you."

Taking her hand, he gently brought them to his lips. "You are more than welcome, my dear."

Lizzy dabbed her eyes. "If you wish it, sir, your sons would be more than welcome to accompany us."

The professor turned from Emily. "Why, yes, I had not thought of bringing them, but they are good boys and would cause no trouble. I see no reason why not."

Emily nodded. "I would welcome them, sir—a pleasant diversion to be sure."

"Mrs Haworth would not object?"

"Oh, no," said Lizzy assuredly, "Lavenia is *one of us*."

He nodded. "Very well, then." He stood. "I will inform Stuart and Charles. Excuse me."

Emily stood, clasping her hands. "Wilhelm," she paused, "I was thinking, under the circumstances, it not being a joyous occasion and all, perhaps the choice should be left to them."

He thought for a moment. "Very well, Miss Emily, I shall ask." He nodded. "Indeed, how very kind of you, my dear."

After leaving the room, Lizzy's eyes widened. "Em, I am very grateful Wilhelm is coming with us. I do not know exactly how Lavenia will take the news."

"I know, Lizzy. In her delicate condition ... I do worry." Shaking her head, she sighed heavily. "I will have to tell her very gently."

"Be sure to have Wilhelm at your side, Em."

"Indeed, I will."

"If Stuart and Charles wish to come along, they shall ride in our carriage, with me, Em. We will stop for Nan. It would be much too crowded with the six of us—I am afraid you will just have to ride alone with Wilhelm."

* * *

Leaving the Meir residence, Lizzy quickly glanced over the professor's sons. Charles sat stoic and well behaved, his suit well pressed, his great overcoat and shoes neat—somewhere in between boy and man. And he seemed pliant enough not even to be bothered that his clothes were obviously selected by his father—his soft blond hair, curled about each ear.

Eyeing Stuart, she noticed the part in his wild bright red hair was crooked. She smiled at herself thinking that he already had a mind of his own—a whimsical sort of mind blending perfectly with his impish little nose, freckled and pert. Was he a mould of his mother?

As Lizzy's carriage stopped in front of the Doddridge townhouse, she sighed. "Do come in, I must break the news of my uncle's demise to our nanny."

"If it is of no matter, Miss Doddridge, we'll just remain here."

"Very well, then."

Lizzy hurried into the house, and within the hour she and Nan emerged.

Settling into the carriage, Nan gave the boys a quick glance over. "You may call me Nana." Her voice was the usual grandmother-in-charge voice, but her soft, crinkly blue eyes belied the gruffness of her manner. Perhaps it was her eighty years on this earth and that she had seen many deaths—the eventual immortality of everyone had hardened her acceptance of the reality. She took Lizzy's hand. "It was kind you of you to stop for me, Lizzy."

"You so loved Uncle Doddridge, Nan. How could I not? You are family, after all. And besides, I need you. I've missed you so."

"Drivel, my dear, drivel. You must harden that heart. I'm afraid you'll squander those tender thoughts on the wrong sorts."

"Oh, hush, Nan." Shaking her head, Lizzy winked at the boys. "Pay her no mind, young men, "she's a mush pot, to be sure."

Stuart smiled politely with a nod.

"Indeed," said Charles not quite so convinced.

"Miss Doddridge," Stuart pointed out the window, "there is where Mr Flannigan lives."

"Stuart, you really must behave, or I shall tell Father."

"I was only pointing to where the musician lives."

Charles's face turned pink. Putting his hands over his mouth, he tried to hide a giggle. Clearing his throat, he leaned into his brother and corrected him with a whisper, "Mr Flannigan is a mortician, Stuart. Not a musician."

Stuart's face puckered. "I beg your pardon, Miss Doddridge."

"I can understand the confusion young man. They do sound very similar."

Stuart smiled up into Lizzy's face. "Do you think Father will marry your sister, Miss Doddridge?"

Charles kicked his brother's foot. "Stuart, you must mind your manners. Father cannot marry again." He shot a glance at Lizzy and then to Nan.

Quickly looking away, Lizzy wondered why he felt that way. *Perhaps the death of his mother was still heavy on the professor's heart.* Cocking her head, she blurted, "I do not understand, Charles. Cannot or wishes not, to marry again?"

"*Cannot*, Miss Doddridge."

Nan squirmed in her seat. "You seem to be very firm with your words, young man. And why *cannot* your father marry whom he wishes?"

"Because our mother has not been buried yet."

* * *

Arriving at Neatham Park, Stuart sat up attentively. "What a silly black dog you have, Miss Doddridge." With his nose pressed hard against the carriage window, he giggled.

"Dog?" Lizzy cocked her head in wonder. "Why, we have no black dog at Neatham."

"There," he pointed, "she has come to greet you, the fine black retriever."

Lizzy snuggled next to Stuart and peered out. "Dear me, God in heaven, it's Holly!"

She anxiously fumbled with the doorknob, but Charles quickly grabbed her hand. "Nay, Miss Doddridge, the carriage is still moving."

"But it is my beloved Holly."

He struck the ceiling panel with his fist and shouted to the groom. "Stop the carriage."

As it slowed, Lizzy flung open the door and jumped out. "Holly, come, girl."

Charles and Stuart jumped out right behind her.

Holly wiggled about her in frenzied delight, licking her face, whining at her miraculous find.

"Oh, girl," she cried. "Oh, girl, how did you find home?" She examined her carefully. "I see your neck has healed very well."

"Really, Miss Doddridge, your lovely frock is becoming terribly soiled," said Charles trying to restrain the dog.

"Nay, she will calm, Charles, she will calm."

Stuart was in the middle of it all. "Her name is Holly, Miss Doddridge?" He stroked her silky head, cooing at her as Lizzy did. She licked his face too. Laughing heartily, he cried, "She is a fondly sort of dog, to be sure!"

"Indeed she is," said Charles. "She has missed you, Miss Doddridge."

Emily's lips pursed. "She has run away, possibly from London. I have not seen her in well over a month."

"Holy fish, London is it? What luck you have, miss."

"Indeed, I do." Hugging Holly, Lizzy wiped her eyes. "She was taken in a spirit of meanness."

Charles's jaw dropped. "Taken? What a despicable act, Miss Doddridge."

Lizzy snuggled the grateful dog to her chest. "I shall not let her go again, I assure you." She stepped up into the carriage. "I am going to walk from here, Nan. Care to join us?"

"Oh, very well," she poked Stuart with her cane, "but keep that hound from my feet, young man."

"Oh, indeed, Madam Nana."

A wee smile crossed her lips. "Humph, Madam Nana, indeed."

Charles called out to the groom. "Move on."

Lizzy and Nan meandered the quarter mile toward the Great House. They caught sight of Wilhelm and Emily waiting on the carriage porch.

"Emily's face looks strained and worn," said Nan.

Stuart broke away and ran toward the woods throwing sticks for Holly. The professor called out to him, but he was much too busy running and playing to pay him any mind.

"I will fetch him, Father," said Charles as he broke into a run.

"Go with him, Lizzy. I shall join Emily," said Nan.

"I won't be long." Lizzy quickly caught up to Charles. Together they watched Stuart frolic in the leaves.

"It has been a long time since I have seen Stuart so lively, Miss Doddridge."

"But you have many dogs, Charles."

"Yes, but a small yard, Miss Doddridge. Our nanny has forbidden us from playing with them in the house. As to the outside, well, the walks are so crowded anymore." He glanced about the wide expanse of Neatham Park, the pastures, oak and poplar trees, the ponds and stables. "You have horses, sheep, cows ... I do love animals."

"You must become a veterinarian then, like your father, Charles." She glanced back at the professor.

"No, ma'am, I mean to become a medical doctor." He brought his hands up and stared at his pinkish milk-white fingers. "I wish to cure the typhoid."

Stunned at such a serious endeavour, Lizzy nodded thinking of Sir Edward. "Noble indeed, Charles. And what prompted such lofty aspirations?"

"My mother, Miss Doddridge."

She studied his sweet profile. "I am terribly sorry, Charles, that your mother died." She thought of her not yet buried ... *I must ask him. What does he mean not yet buried?*

"Ma'am?"

"Yes, Charles."

"I believe my father is happy."

She glanced back at her sister and Wilhelm.

"I think you are correct, Charles. And I am very happy for it."

"But you look so sad."

Lizzy sighed deeply. "It is just that we must tell our dear cousin that our uncle has passed on. And I don't relish the task."

He nodded with sadness. "I know very well the feeling."

Stuart ran up to them, Holly at his side, her tongue hanging to the side, panting.

"Stuart, we must join Father now. Do not run away again. This is a sombre day."

He bowed his little head. "I forgot," he said poking the mud with a stick.

When they all reached the porch, Emily held a sad little smile. "Lizzy, dare I believe that is Holly?"

"It is, she must have run away, for no wonder."

Wilhelm sighed. "My son is ecstatic to be running once more—in the cool fresh country air, with a dog, in the tall field grass. It is a healing balm for his heart, and I must say, mine."

Emily rubbed her arms. "A healing balm, indeed, sir."

"You must bring him here often, sir," said Lizzy with a warm smile.

"I should like that too, sir," said Charles nodding emphatically.

Nan quipped, "It may take a while, but I shall *warm* to the idea."

"We have missed you, Nan," said Emily with a sigh. Her face was pale, her eyes rimmed red. "Well, then," she turned and entered the house, "we have Lavenia and the servants to speak with." She put her arm around Nan. "Come along, dearest."

Mr Maxwell, Mary, and Helen stood in the vestibule as they entered. Holly squirmed in between everyone.

Looking about the fresh new faces, Mr Maxwell hemmed. "And where is Mr Doddridge, Miss Emily?"

"Excuse me, Mr Maxwell. Lizzy, will you please show our guests into the drawing room. I shan't be long."

Emily, Mr Maxwell, Mary, Helen, and Nan slowly disappeared down the hall to gather the rest of the servants.

* * *

The evening tapers had not been attended, and the drawing room was growing darker by the minute. "Excuse me while I light the candles," said Lizzy. She took a strip of paper and held it to the flames in the fireplace.

Stuart jumped to her side. "May I, Miss Doddridge? Please? Father allows me to light the candles at home." He glanced at him for permission. The professor nodded.

"Very well, then. All of them, Stuart, please."

Mary entered the room; her nose and eyes were red. "Excuse the unlit room, Miss Lizzy."

"Do not worry over it, Mary," said Lizzy in a low tone. "We are quite capable."

"Is there anything I may bring you, ma'am?"

"Perhaps tea, Mary." Lizzy set down her candle. "Where is Mrs Haworth?"

Wiping her eyes with the tip of her apron, she said, "In her room, Miss Lizzy. Miss Emily instructed us to wait until she comes down. We were told not to say a word."

Thinking of Charles and Stuart's feelings, Emily had a private word with Wilhelm, and the boys were shown into the library.

Before they left, Lizzy pulled Stuart aside. "I would be most appreciative if you would entertain Holly this evening."

His face lit up. "Indeed, Miss Doddridge."

Charles stepped forward. "A pleasure, Miss Doddridge."

"Thank you, both." She smiled warmly. "Holly will love the company, I am sure."

* * *

The mantle clock in the study struck eight soft gongs. Emily and Wilhelm were sitting near the hearth. Nan stood at the window when Lavenia and Lizzy entered.

Lavenia moved slowly wincing at every step, her face flushed and swollen, her eyes red. She took to her favourite easy chair, and in clumsy fashion, sat down. "How was the wedding?"

Lizzy put a pillow at her back. "Dear girl, it will soon be over."

"Soon is not soon enough." Lavenia wrinkled her nose. "Tell me, how did you find the wedding of the century?"

The professor coughed.

Lavenia jolted at hearing him. "Oh, dear me, Professor Meir, sir, forgive my rudeness. Why, I did not see you there."

He half-bowed. "Do not worry over formalities, Mrs Haworth." Glancing at her, his brows knit. "You have more to worry about than me. You are most uncomfortable, ma'am?"

She nodded. "Oh, indeed. Forgive me for being so cross. I cannot tell you how uncomfortable I am."

Emily knelt on the floor and gently removed Lavenia's slippers. "Let me rub your feet, love. Poor dear, they are so swollen. I will have Mary bring a basin of water. You must soak them."

Closing her eyes, Lavenia nodded. "Oh, yes," she sighed deeply, "what a lovely idea."

"Why, that chair you are in must be very uncomfortable," said Nan looking concerned. "You must sit up or lay flat."

"Oh, indeed, Lavenia," said Emily, "let us remove to your room. We shall make you comfortable there."

Trying to sit up, Lavenia nodded. "Very well, but wait, will you?" She tried to push herself up, but fell back. "Oh, I can not—perhaps if I just rest here a moment longer."

Emily wrung her hands. "Lizzy, be a dear and have Mary warm a basin of water for Lavenia."

"Very well." She tugged on the rope pull. Sensing something more than water being needed, Lizzy exchanged worried glances with Nan.

"Move her to the day nursery," said Nan. "She'll be more comfortable there." Emily read her serious face. "Oh, indeed, Nan, she will not have to walk such a distance, and there is a lovely day bed there."

Wilhelm moved to Lavenia's side. "Splendid idea, allow me to me help you."

When Mary entered, Emily instructed her to prepare the nursery, fetch another basin of warm water, and build a strong fire. "Mrs Haworth is not feeling well, Mary, please hurry."

Mary took one look at the pale, perspiring Lavenia and gulped.

Emily pressed her hand. "Hurry along now, Mary, and do as I say."

"Yes, ma'am."

Wilhelm felt Lavenia's brow. Beads of sweat dripped down the side of her face. Removing his handkerchief, he dabbed her brow. "She is cool to the touch."

Mary scurried back in; her face ashen, her voice quivering, "A Mr Flannigan is here."

Lavenia read Mary's worried face. "Who is Mr Flannigan Mary, and why are you crying?"

Wilhelm interrupted, "I shall attend Mr Flannigan, Miss Emily." He hurried to Mary. Taking her elbow, he escorted her from the room.

"Why is Mary crying?" asked Lavenia as she tried to sit up.

Nan patted her hand. "Oh, Mary is always the one to have fits now and again. Pay her no mind."

"That's right, Lavenia," said Lizzy fighting to keep her own *fits* at bay. "Come now let us go into the nursery where you may lie down."

The sisters led her down the hall into the nursery.

Helen bustled in. "The water is on the hob, Miss Emily. I'll bring it when it's ready."

"There now, Lavenia, dear," said Emily spreading a day quilt over her. "Do make yourself comfortable or at least try."

"Thank you, all."

Just outside, in the courtyard, there could be heard the bustling of people with cries and low murmurs of all sorts. A carriage came and went. The clopping of horse's hooves striking the cobbles echoed in muted tones.

"What is happening?" said Lavenia. "And where is Uncle? Something has happened to Uncle ... please, you must tell me."

Emily took a deep breath and closed her eyes. "Uncle has passed on, dearest."

"Oh, no," she cried bringing her hands to her face, "such dreadful news."

"Just outside the Cathedral, after the wedding," whispered Emily.

"It was a natural death, Cousin," said Lizzy through tears. "It has been a dreadful day, Lavenia. We have tried to be as brave as possible, but alas, the grief comes."

"Yes, I understand, I understand," said Lavenia trying to comfort Emily and Lizzy. "Do not fret over me a moment longer, you have worried enough."

She made a motion to rise, but Nan pressed her shoulder. "No, you must remain quiet."

Emily wiped her eyes. "Indeed, together we must be steadfast and strong. There is much to be done."

"Oh, indeed, but what are we to do, Emily?" said Lavenia.

Wilhelm was with us when Uncle ... when he passed on. He has been such a gentleman, such a kind thoughtful man, Cousin."

"Indeed, right this moment he is with Mr Flannigan, the mortician from London."

"Flannigan?" said Lavenia, "indeed, Mr Flannigan he was our neighbour." She dabbed her eyes. "I know him, but slightly."

"He is supposed to be an excellent mortician, dearest," assured Emily. "Indeed, the same fellow who handled the affairs of Wilhelm's wife."

Lizzy spoke up, "Wilhelm's son, Charles, informed me that his mother died of the typhoid. He has two boys yet living at home, Charles and Stuart. They are upstairs at present.

Entering the room, Mary carried a basin of hot water. "Here you are, ma'am." Setting it on the table, she sighed. "Professor Meir is in the hallway, Miss Emily. He requests to speak with you and Miss Lizzy."

"Lavenia, may Wilhelm come in?" asked Emily.

"Oh, but of course." She wiped her eyes and slicked back her hair. "Yes, indeed, see him in, Mary."

Wilhelm entered the small nursery. Along one wall sat a shiny mahogany bassinette, white netting casually draped over it. A small white cradle sat on the floor next to it. Little muslin blankets were folded neatly and stacked about the end tables. Embroidered baby clothes were laid out on a small changing table. Lizzy and Emily's old baby toys were stashed away in a box, a warm fire burned in the hearth.

Emily whispered to the professor that they had informed Lavenia of Uncle's demise.

Looking grim, he knelt at Lavenia's side and took her hand. "Mrs Haworth, my deepest condolences at the passing of your beloved uncle." He turned his attention to Lizzy and Emily. "Regarding Mr Doddridge, everything will soon be ready."

"Thank you, Professor Meir," said Lavenia.

"Madam," he took her pulse, "you are near your time, I am most positive."

She rubbed her stomach and lurched forward. "God in heaven ... any moment, indeed!" She gasped, her eyes glazed over. "It is coming now!"

"I believe you, madam." Glancing at Emily, he whispered, "The baby is coming. Hurry along now and bring me very much hot water, clean muslin ... and keep the room warm."

She gulped. "Certainly, sir."

Hearing Lavenia's half-cry, half-moan, they hurriedly left searching for Mary and Helen. Flinging open the kitchen door, Emily cried, "Mrs Haworth is having her baby!" Her eyes were wide and red. "Oh, boil more water."

"And we need clean muslin, Mary, immediately. The professor and Nan are with her," said Lizzy.

"Are they still in the nursery, ma'am?"

"Yes, hurry along now, Mary."

Grabbing the kettle, she called back to Helen, "bring all the clean muslin you can find."

Hurrying from the kitchen, Emily and Lizzy bumped into Mr Flannigan—a tall, thin man with thick, black, bushy eyebrows; his arms very much longer than his waistcoat sleeves. He removed his hat; his voice was deep and raspy. "May I be of assistance?"

Lizzy stammered, frightened by the ghoulish looking man, "Oh, God no, go away!" She pulled her hand from Emily's and ran toward the nursery.

"Oh, do forgive her, Mr Flannigan," said Emily. "Our cousin is delivering a baby at the moment, Professor Meir is to help."

"Indeed, perhaps I may be able to assist." He followed her to the nursery door and stopped as Mary pushed past him carrying bolts of cloth.

The professor spotted him. "Flannigan, come this instant. I need you."

Nan had ripped sheets of muslin and stacked them on the nearby table. "Emily, use these to dab her brow."

Lizzy stood wringing her hands and praying.

"We will need more water," said the professor. Glancing at Lizzy's pale, distorted face, he shook his head. "Miss Elizabeth, better you see how my sons are doing, I would appreciate it very much."

Gulping air, she nodded. "Very well, sir." She hurried around Flannigan, refusing to look him in the eye and bounded up the steps. Bolting into the library, she closed the door behind her. "God in heaven."

Charles leapt from his chair, tossing his book aside. "Oh, Miss Doddridge, what could the matter be?"

"My cousin, Mrs Haworth, is having a baby."

"At this very moment, miss?"

Nodding, she slid slowly to the floor.

Holly jumped on top of her, whining and licking her face. Stuart knelt beside her. "Oh, Miss Doddridge, please do not cry so."

Charles glanced around the room and spied a decanter full of something amber. He poured her a glass. "Here you are, Miss Doddridge," he sniffed the drink and wrinkled his nose.

Lizzy emptied the glass and handed it back to him. "Help me up, will you?"

"Yes, ma'am."

Now standing, she held her head in her hands. "Do forgive me; it is the sight of blood."

Charles stiffened. "Blood? Then Father must need me, Miss Doddridge."

"No, Charles. Emily is there, the maids are there, your father is there, Nan is there, Mr Flannigan is there."

"Mr Flannigan?" Stuart's little face screwed up into a question mark. "What would he know to do?"

* * *

There came a light tap at the library door, Emily and Meir entered. The clock, at that exact moment struck eleven. Stuart was curled up on the chaise with Holly, sound asleep. Charles was sitting in Uncle Doddridge's favourite over-stuffed chair, an open book on his lap, his head resting sideways, asleep.

Lizzy was staring at the fire when the door opened. Holly's ears perked. Glancing up, she could not, right off, read Emily's face, it held such a look. Sitting up abruptly, she pushed back her hair. Rubbing her eyes, she whispered, "Emily, what is wrong?"

Emily's face, even in the warm glow of the hearth fire, was gaunt. Her large brown eyes remained cast down, her lashes moist and twisted. Her complexion usually pink, more recently red by association with Wilhelm, was now pale. She held Uncle's Bible. She muttered something.

Lizzy sat up, straining to hear her sister. "What was that you said, Em?"

"The baby survived, Lizzy. He is a fine boy."

The professor held Emily steady. Nodding, he half-smiled. "Indeed, a fine boy."

Holly, unusually calm, jumped up on the sofa and sat by Lizzy's side.

Emily slowly approached and stroked her head. "Good girl, Holly."

Lizzy brought Emily's soft, warm hand to her cheek. Closing her eyes, she felt the wetness of her tears. "Emily, please tell me."

Wilhelm softly cleared his throat and whispered, "Lavenia has died, Elizabeth."

* * *

The next morning at Neatham Park was a ghastly family affair. The Doddridge family plot was made ready for Lavenia; she would be laid to rest next to her beloved Aunt Lucille and

Uncle Henry. The grave was mounded with fresh black clods of disturbed soil that stuck up majestically through the winter's first snow. A light dusting from the west sprinkled the headstones of Emily and Lizzy's mother and father.

Charles proudly held an umbrella over Emily and his father. Stuart stood on a rather large stone, and while bracing himself on his brother's shoulder, held an umbrella over Lizzy. The wind was blowing, the clouds dark and lugubrious—the stark, jagged brownish-black trees swayed cold and naked. Helen and Mary held each other and wept quietly as Flannigan remained stoic by their side. He did not have an umbrella.

The vicar, Mr Smythe, parted the air with his hands. "Amen."

As everyone followed the vicar back to the Great House, Stuart took his father's hand. "Father, are we to bury Mother like that someday?"

Emily stopped abruptly. Squeezing Lizzy's hand, she bowed her head.

Nan frowned at Stuart with a questioning look.

With his black robe billowing, Mr Smythe turned back and glared at Stuart. "I beg your pardon, young man?"

"My wife was cremated, sir." Wilhelm's face was strained and pale. "We have her ashes in a cloisonné urn."

The vicar stood motionless, his brows raised as if stunned at such a revelation. "Cremated, sir?"

"Indeed, Mr Smythe. The Queen's own personal physician, Sir Henry Thompson, has fostered the practice."

"The typhoid, if you must know, is the very reason," said Nan challenging the vicar to dare voice his disdain again.

Charles and Stuart gathered at their father's side. Stuart looked up at his father, "And someday, Father, Mother will be buried too."

"Yes, my son, very soon. Very soon."

Chapter 7 – Professor Meir Offers a Proposal

London
Wilhelm proposed to Emily one quiet, early evening, while they sat in front of the fire in the drawing room at Neatham Park. Lizzy was in the next room reading to Charles and Stuart, Holly slept contentedly on the hearthrug at the bottom of her feet. The late winter air sifted through the slightly open window and brought an airy lightness to the otherwise stuffy room.

"My dear Emily," said Wilhelm as he took her hand, "I have a splendid little option … a bibelot in my vest pocket that I wish to place into your hands. Do be kind in your response."

"Dear me, Wilhelm, must you be so dramatic?" She giggled. "Very well, let me see my splendid option that you are hiding—your little bibelot."

He fumbled about his vest pocket. "Why, it was just here … ." He patted every pocket and then, in despair, sighed deeply. "Dear me, I must have somehow misplaced it. Oh, how could I have done such a thing?"

"Wilhelm, could this be it?" In the palm of her hand sat a small box, neatly wrapped in brown paper. "It was lying just here. It's a wonder you did not sit on it." She examined it closer. "Aha, Charles must have wrapped such a neat package. String dangled from the box. A half bow dangled down the side. "And, Stuart must have tied the bow."

He smiled, his monocle set firm over his left eye. "Oh, my dear, you are so clever this evening."

"I must agree, Wilhelm." She slowly untied the string and removed the crinkly brown paper, and within sat a white box.

"So, I am to open it and tell you if I will accept it? And if I do not, you will flail about like a fish?"

"Now you've got it, darling. Please do open it. The boys and I are all a wiggle over your ... ah, your approval." He moved closer, twitching excitedly. "Do go on, dear, it won't bite you."

Emily held it up. "Well, it is very light, sir, I dare say. Perhaps I shall open it in the morning," she teased. "Oh, very well, yes, I will accept it."

"But you must first open it, Emily dearest. One cannot just say *yes*."

"She lifted the lid and her eyes flooded with tears. "Wilhelm, this ... this is no trinket, sir." She jumped up and put her arms around his neck and kissed him. "This is an exquisite ... more than exquisite ring."

"Put it on, my dear." Tears rimmed his eyes. "I do hope it fits."

She slipped the magnificent diamond silver filigreed ring onto her finger and shook her head in wonder. "Of course I shall keep the ring, but to your option to wed or not to wed, if that is the only option, then of course, I must say ... no."

"Very well," he pulled her close, "we shall marry in July."

* * *

Cradling Lavenia's baby, Lizzy reassured Emily, and quite emphatically, "You must marry him sooner than later. Six months mourning is quite enough time for Uncle and Lavenia. They would want it so."

"I know dearest, but I ..."

"Emily, I will not hear another word of it. You must marry Wilhelm. Go away on a wonderful honeymoon. I will be perfectly fine at Neatham Park. I have much yet to do with the final reassembly of the conservatory here, I have the baby, I will have Charles and Stuart to keep me company, and I have Nan. I even imagine his other children—all eight of them will come a visiting." She laughed. "Neatham Park has probably never seen so much activity."

Holly sat up and pawed the air.

"Oh, yes," Emily laughed and ruffled her head, "she has you too."

Wilhelm entered the study. "So, what is the decision?"

Emily beamed. "The sixth day of July, sir."

A broad smile crossed his face, holding his hands in prayerful assembly, he said, "Amen."

Emily, in a rare moment of showy affection, put her arms around Wilhelm's neck and kissed his mouth. "As you wish it, sir, July 6, my love, we shall be married."

Taking her in his arms, they danced about the room. Lizzy, still cradling the baby, joined them.

* * *

Lizzy was giving Charles his piano lessons when Helen interrupted. Holding the silver mail salver, she apologised, "Beg pardon, Miss Elizabeth, but the courier just brought this letter."

Lifting her fingers from the piano keys, Lizzy looked at the letter. "Indeed," she looked puzzled, "it is addressed to me."

"Yes, ma'am."

Lizzy frowned. "Belgium? I know no one in Belgium, Helen."

She ripped it open.

1 July 1871 – Brussels
Dear Miss Elizabeth,

I have some very sad news, indeed. I just learned this morning, in a passing conversation with Lady Beatrice, that Holly had escaped her care many months ago, late November, apparently. I apologise, you must think me quite uncaring, but I assure you, Miss Elizabeth, I had no idea of Lady Beatrice's great affections for Holly nor that she was to be brought along on our honeymoon. Forgive me the words that I wrote to your uncle requesting you look in on Holly—I pray your good and great understanding. If you wish it, I shall have Professor Meir scour the city to find her ... truly I say to you, I am sorry. We will be returning to London sometime in August, perhaps, or a little later. Please send my best regards to Mr Doddridge, and of course your sister, Miss Doddridge.

Sincerely, Sir Edward North

July 21, 1871 – Neatham Park

Dear Sir Edward,

It is with great sadness, sir, that I inform you of our beloved Uncle Doddridge's sudden passing. And, it is with equal sadness that I also share that our most beloved cousin, Mrs Rupert Haworth, died the very same day. She was with child and went into immediate labour here at Neatham Park—we supposed from the shock of Uncle's demise. Our cousin Lavenia was a very delicate creature, sir, but there are always the miracles that somehow intertwine our sorrows—two such miracles have blessed me, Sir. Lavenia's child, a beautiful, healthy boy, survived and Holly found her way home. I cannot tell you the joy the child and the dog have brought into my world of profound grief and sorrow. I shall await your coming before returning Holly to Tillyard Lodge, if that suits you, sir.

I will share with you a refreshing new beginning, Sir Edward. My beloved sister and Professor Meir wed in July. You must find it quite shocking—the age difference, but they are deliriously happy, I assure you. His youngest two, Stuart and Charles are staying with me here at Neatham Park while Wilhelm and Emily tour Italy on their honeymoon. I have taken the liberty Sir, of treading on Tillyard Lodge to show the boys Phoebe's colt—he is growing into a magnificent animal, sir.

I am saddened to have shared the distressing news, but heartened with words of joy regarding the child, Holly, Phoebe's baby, and my sister's wedded bliss. I hope I have found you, as well, sir, and in wedded bliss.

Yours most truly,
Miss Elizabeth Doddridge

Folding the letter, Lizzy held it to her lips. "I take that back about your wedded bliss, Sir Edward."

"I beg your pardon, Miss Lizzy?" Helen stoked the fire. "Did you say something to me, miss?"

"No," Lizzy sighed and slid the letter into its envelope. "I was just being what Emily would call, wicked."

"Indeed, Miss Lizzy." She smiled at her fondly. "You are the last person I would ever call wicked."

"Thank you, Helen." She handed her the letter. "Please have this taken to Bentley to be posted."

Holly lay stretched out on the daybed, lifting her head, she thumped her tail once and licked Lizzy's hand, but did not budge. "Oh, did I disturb you, Your Majesty?" Walking toward the nursery, Lizzy turned. "And where have Stuart and Charles gone off to?"

"Master Charles and Master Stuart are in the garden, Miss Lizzy." Helen put the letter in her apron. "Would you that I find them?"

Hearing the baby fuss, Lizzy shook her head. "No, no. I shall tend the baby and then take the air."

Slipping off the sofa, Holly loped alongside and followed her into the nursery. Lizzy heard him cooing and watched as his little hands flailed about the air. "So, my little man," she tweaked his chin, "you have awoken from your nap, have you?" Lifting him, she kissed his smooth pink skin. Cradling his wobbly little head, she smiled, half-giggling, "Oh, how I love you." Holly nudged her leg. "Yes, I love you too, Holly."

Glancing out the window, Lizzy noticed the Meir boys out taking the air. *How well-behaved they are and without a mother's touch; a mother's guiding hand; someone to make sure their hair is combed, their faces clean and fresh, their teeth washed.*

She thought of her own motherless world and hugged the child, kissing his forehead. *I suppose Emily and I have done quite well, but then we had each other. Yes*, she watched the brothers walk about the garden, *and now they have Emily, lucky enough for them.* Cradling the baby, she looked down into his expectant gaze. *And you shall have me.*

Hearing shouts, Lizzy looked up. Charles waved, and she waved back—Stuart was busy jumping a small kew hedgerow. Removing from the window, Lizzy changed the baby and wrapped him securely within his little blue and yellow patch quilt. "I think, young man, we shall take a walk in the conservatory before your meal. I want to see how the Millers are doing in its reconstruction."

Holly whined. "Yes, you may come along."

Stepping out into the warm summer air, Lizzy snuggled the baby closer as the boys approached her.

Charles grinned.

Squinting in the sunshine, Lizzy said, "I take it you have been busy enough, Charles?

Stuart giggled. "Charlie was picking you a bouquet, Miss Lizzy."

His face reddened.

"Rocking the baby, she smiled. "How dear of you, Charles." She glanced around, "Where is it?"

Stuart bolted from her side, calling back, "In the conservatory, Miss Lizzy."

"Stuart," cried Charles, "don't disturb the flowers or I will knuckle your head."

"Well, then, Charles, I must go see what sort of bouquet you have made."

He held the opaque glass door as Lizzy stepped into the conservatory. She walked lightly over the white stone floor to the wicker chairs. Sitting, she acted quite the surprised recipient when he handed her the flowers.

"Indeed, pink rosebuds, what a lovely bouquet." The baby began to fuss, and this time no matter what she did, he continued to wail. "Dear me," she handed the flowers to Charles, "do either of you know a lullaby you might sing to quiet our dearest cousin?"

Jumping up and down wildly, Stuart shouted, "I do, I do." And he began a loud cacophony of sounds.

"A soothing refrain, Stuart," pleaded Charles, "you'll wake the dead with that." Quickly covering his mouth, "Beg your pardon, Miss Lizzy."

Suddenly the baby quit crying. Stuart grinned. Pulling his baggy trousers up, he darted from the conservatory with Holly in fast pursuit.

Lizzy nudged Charles. "Why not join him? There's a wonderful lake out back where you may fish, throw stones, climb ... ."

"Really, Miss Lizzy? I would love to fish." Looking down at his trousers, he sighed. "Oh, but I do not have the proper clothes."

"Do not fret so, Charles, we shall clean them if they soil. Go now and find Jacob the gardener, he shall give you everything you need."

"Oh, thank you, Miss Lizzy. Father and I used to fish."

"Well, then, you must bring us supper." Just as he was to run out, she stopped him. "I thank you for the sweet bouquet, Charles. That was very thoughtful of you." She kissed his cheek.

"Indeed, you are welcome," he said blushing. And with a half-bow, he hurriedly ran helter-skelter toward the garden house shouting for his brother and Holly.

"Miss Lizzy," said Mary entering the room. "May I take the baby? It's near his feeding time."

Glancing about Sir Edward's near finished reconstructed conservatory, Lizzy shook her head. "No, I shall feed him here, Mary. Set the tea table there." She gestured. Inhaling deeply, she kissed the baby's forehead. "It is such a lovely day."

"Very well, ma'am."

Hearing someone behind her, Lizzy turned. "Ah, there you are, Mr Miller."

Wiping his rough, mud-stained hands on his trousers, he glanced around at the conservatory from Tillyard Lodge. "Near completed, Miss Doddridge." He looked well pleased. "My sons are almost finished with the porticos and walls in the back."

Staring up into the glass ceiling, she nodded. "Yes, it is coming along quite nicely."

"We only have to attach the glass to that wall and put in a ..." he scratched his head, "a secret passage, Miss Doddridge?"

"Well, not exactly a secret passage, Mr Miller—just inconspicuous. You must remember Lady Marlboro's entrance from the inner courtyard. Do you not?"

"Lady Marlboro?" He thought for a moment. "Oh," he nodded, "indeed, Tillyard Lodge's passage, the one into Dr North's conservatory. You want it just as he had it. Yes, it was rather clever in its design, ma'am."

"Yes, and that is exactly what I want." The baby began to fuss. Rocking the child on her hip, she continued, "Mr Miller, do show me your ideas before you begin, will you?"

"Oh, indeed, Miss Doddridge, that I will."

Mary buzzed about the table fixing baby Edward's meal. Bread, soaking in warm milk sat in a little porcelain saucer covered with a napkin; a dash of plum pudding in a tiny bowl; Edward's tiny silver spoon half-hidden beneath his dish.

"There now, Miss Lizzy," said Mary still fussing with the white lace tablecloth, "everything is set."

"And this little man is hungry." Glancing once more around the warm, moist room, Lizzy sniffed the air, hugged the baby and watched Mr Miller leave.

Uncurling the baby's little fists, she teased, "Hungry?" His tiny hands waved wildly. Dipping the spoon into the soggy warm bread, Lizzy tasted it first. "Mmm, just right." She touched his mouth with the tip of the spoon and parted his lips. Squirming now, his busy little fingers moved as if playing a piano—his eyes intently focused on Lizzy's lips.

"I love you."

"Beg pardon, Miss Lizzy." Mary interrupted, her face drawn; her voice hoarse.

"What is it, Mary?"

"Mr Haworth has come." She wiped her brow with her apron. "And he wishes to see you."

"Rupert? Oh, God in heaven, Mary. Her face drained. What could he possibly want?" She sat down and then stood. "Oh, God in Heaven, very well, then, show him in."

Mary's eyes were wide and fearful. "Bring him here, Miss Lizzy?"

Nervously spooning the mushy bread into the baby's anxious mouth, Lizzy shrugged. "Yes, yes." She exhaled heavily. "I suppose so."

Haworth entered the side yard holding his hat, and in his usual swagger, followed Mary into the conservatory.

Lizzy quickly turned her back. *I even detest watching him walk.*

"Good afternoon, Miss Lizzy."

Twisting in her chair, she corrected him, "In future, sir, you will address me as Miss Doddridge." Glancing at his cigar, she huffed, "And I do not allow smoking at Neatham Park."

His face reddened. "Pardon me." He stuck the smouldering cigar into Lizzy's revered Eliza rose bush.

She gasped.

Mary rushed to the pot and immediately removed the muddied cigar and carried it outside.

Rupert ignored the servant. "I have come to see Lavenia's grave."

"Indeed." Lizzy held the baby protectively. "Had I only known you were coming, I would have dressed the child appropriately."

He shrugged. "The child means nothing to me, I assure you. I have only come to visit the grave, to condole with my wife."

Lizzy's brows furrowed in anger. "The baby means nothing?" She glared. "And you do not wish to even see him, hold him? Why, I do not even suppose you know his name?"

Holding her gaze, he shook his head. "And why should I? Nothing of yours holds any interest to me."

Mary entered with the footman, Mr Watson, and Mr Miller. His sons stood back a few feet—hammers in hand.

Lizzy closed her eyes. *God Almighty, he does not know. He does not know Lavenia was with child ... .* Glancing down at the baby, Lizzy kissed his forehead. Little white milk bubbles were about his lips, his arms flailing for more. *I must tell Rupert you are his son.*

Suddenly the door to the conservatory opened.

A young girl, in cheap clothes, heavily rouged and with charcoaled eyes sauntered to his side. "Rupe, what's takin' you?" Glancing about the room, she sighed. "Well, well now, this is a money place all right." Sniffing the air, she sauntered to the baby's silver bowl. "Indeed, Rupe, this is a real money place, so it is." She approached Lizzy. "I love 'em babies, miss." Leaning over the child, she smiled. "I 'av four meself."

Lizzy smelled alcohol on the tramp and shirked. "Refrain from touching the baby or I'll ... ."

"I weren't going to touch your baby, miss. I swear it." Her gnarly yellow teeth were dull and jagged, her lips, puffy.

Mary hurried to Lizzy's side, her arms open. "I'll take him, Miss Lizzy."

"No, Mary." She snuggled the fussing baby to her shoulder, patting him as he began to cry.

"Humph," said the strumpet of a girl, "sounds like me own, so he does. They're always cryin' and screamin' never enough to fill 'em potbellies is what methinks."

"Shut up, Charlotte," said Rupert, "shut up and go back to the carriage."

"What?" She frowned, "But Rupe you wanted me to see this fancy place." She pouted. Glancing at Lizzy, she shrugged. "I wear me finest frock; comes me all this way and he shouts at me like a dog."

Lizzy glanced at the footman. "Show them the way out, Mr Watson."

"Yes, ma'am."

Rupert removed a cigar from his vest pocket and stuck it in his mouth. "Screaming babies have never suited me." He nodded with an arrogant air and headed for the door.

Talking through tears, Lizzy's voice faltered, "Even, even your own son's, Rupert?"

Mary gasped. "Oh, no, Miss Lizzy, you mustn't tell 'em."

"Quiet, Mary."

"*My* son?" he replied with the cigar clenched between his teeth. A peculiar look spread across his ruddy, pocked marked face. Running his hands through his slick, shiny black hair, he smirked at Charlotte. "Well, well, I have a son."

She shrugged nonchalantly. "We'll take 'em, Rupe." Cackling. "Eh, what's one more to the pot, lovey. No forgettin' his little silver bowl 'n spoon."

"No," cried Lizzy as she tried to calm the now screaming infant, "this child is more than 'one more,' Rupert. For God sakes," she pleaded while the baby wailed, "do one decent thing in your life and leave Neatham Park and never come back." Sitting down abruptly, she brought the baby to the nape of her neck, boldly holding Rupert's insolent gaze. "I sincerely pray to God for your soul, Rupert Haworth."

Lizzy noted that the cruel, defiant glitter in his eyes suddenly vanished—perhaps a spark of human dignity remained yet, but she was not exactly sure.

Removing his cigar, he stared at Lizzy for a brief moment. "Very well, Miss Doddridge," his face now red, perspiration beaded on his brow, "I shall never return to Neatham Park again." He took Charlotte's arm and gestured toward the door. Now standing on the threshold, he turned. "What's its name?"

Lizzy stood, the baby had quit crying. "Edward."

"Thank you, Miss Doddridge." He moved quietly out the door. Charlotte shrugged, briefly glancing at the baby's silver bowl and with a sigh, waved goodbye. "Tata."

Following an impulse, Lizzy hurried to the door. "Rupert." He turned.

"If you would still wish to visit Lavenia's grave, Watson will show you the way."

He nodded. "Indeed, I would. Thank you." He and Charlotte continued out into the courtyard.

Lizzy waved away at the air. "Dear me," she rubbed her nose, "they must never bathe." Handing the baby to Mary, Lizzy wearily sat down. Lowering her head into her hands, she sighed. "Put him down for his nap, will you?"

"Yes, ma'am."

Just then Charles dashed in, smiling proudly as held up a string of fish. His grin suddenly vanished. "What is wrong, Miss Lizzy?" Glancing back over her shoulder at Rupert and Charlotte, he frowned. "Did those strangers say something to upset you, ma'am?"

She smiled sadly. "No, Charles, they have only come to pay their respects to the baby's mother."

"Oh, indeed." His manner softened.

Stuart bounded in, all a breath. His bright red hair now a mass of bouncing curls, he slapped his leg, gawking at the fish. "What a lucky boy Charles is, Miss Lizzy."

"Luck?" She shook her head as she tweaked Stuart's freckled little nose. "Pitch a lucky man into the Nile, and he will come up with a fish in his mouth. Now that is luck, young man."

"Ha ha! So it is, Miss Lizzy."

Charles beamed. "If Stuart and Holly would only have kept still, I would have caught more."

Examining the fish, Lizzy laughed. "That looks enough for a pretty dinner this evening."

"Who were them people, Miss Lizzy?" asked Stuart.

"They have come to pay their respects to baby Edward's mother, Cousin Lavenia."

"Hmm," he murmured. Suddenly his usually sparkly blue eyes clouded, his head lowered as he toyed with the fish. "Thank you, Miss Lizzy, for helping Father bury Mother in a proper cemetery."

Lizzy rubbed his arm. "Indeed."

Charles nodded. "Now we can go visit her properly, without begging Father to show us the jar."

Lizzy closed her eyes. "Grief has a way of fogging one's thinking betimes, do be mindful."

Charles nodded. "Yes, ma'am."

Sniffing the air, Lizzy half-laughed and pulled on the string of fish. "There now, take them to the cook before they curl."

The boys sped off toward the servants' entrance. Holly jumped up for an affectionate rub to the head. "So, you return to me again, is it?" Kneeling down to hug her, she watched as Rupert's carriage ambled out of Neatham Park and onto the London Road. "Thank God they are gone."

Chapter 8 – Haworth's Efforts to Secure his Son

Dashing to the window, Stuart cried, "It is Father, it is Father! They have finally come home from their honeymooning."

Lizzy held the baby to the nape of her neck and joined Charles at the door. The morning haze had burned off, and the sun was now full upon everyone and everything. She waved excitedly. "Welcome home."

Charles bolted from her side and stood anxiously with Stuart as the carriage ambled to a stop—both boys puffed up.

"Sir," Charles beamed, "so good to see you, Father."

Stuart squinted in the bright sun as he took his father's hand. "Indeed, sir."

Embracing his sons, Wilhelm hugged them tenderly. Emily stood on the carriage steps smiling at Lizzy.

"Welcome home." Lizzy blew her a kiss. Tears welled in her eyes. "Oh, how we have missed you."

Nan stood leaning on her cane. "Indeed, it's about time you returned."

The servants made over Wilhelm and Emily with warm words of welcome. Taking their wraps, Helen said they were home just in time for lunch.

"Come in, come in," said Nan as she took Emily's hand and slowly moved into the drawing room. "You must tell me about Italy."

Emily's tan complexion was awash with blushing hues. Her five freckles were now twenty, her sparkling green eyes mature. Her countenance seemed ... content and satisfied.

Lizzy knew by the calm, graceful way her sister now held herself that Wilhelm was quite the man—that she was sure.

"Sir," she took his hand, "you look fit and happy. You both look terribly at ease."

Wilhelm cleared his throat, glancing at his sons, he nodded. "We had an excellent trip, indeed. Next time, Charles and Stuart, you shall come along."

Stuart beamed.

Charles held a happy grin. "Indeed, sir, I should like that, sir."

"Charles caught very many fish, Father."

"Indeed?" Wilhelm bent over his youngest, tapping his chest with his finger. "And did you roast the eyeballs on a stick, like I taught you, Stuart?"

His little face screwed up into a wrinkled ball. He giggled. "Indeed not, Father."

Emily nodded at her new family. "Have they been well-behaved?"

Nan hemmed. "Indeed, the boys have been running and playing every day, mud or dust."

"Italy was more than beautiful." Smiling dreamily at her new husband, she sighed. "We must go back, Wil."

"Indeed, my love. We shall."

"Oh, indeed," said Nan, "and I will come along."

The boys looked at her in puzzlement as everyone laughed.

Taking a seat next to Emily, Lizzy uncovered the baby. With all the commotion little Edward had awakened. He was now trying to focus his tiny black eyes on Emily. She took him in her arms and fluffed his rather longish, black hair. "What a beautiful little boy he is, Lizzy." Sighing, she ran her finger over his soft, pink face. "Such perfect features." She kissed his forehead. "Indeed," she glanced up at Wilhelm, "if he was a girl, I had the honour of naming her Lavenia. If a boy, Lizzy had the honour of naming him. Smiling, she nudged her sister. "And she loved the name Edward."

"And why did you pick the name Edward, Miss Lizzy?" said Charles.

Stuart giggled. "Miss Lizzy must love an Edward, simple that."

Lizzy's blush deepened, glancing quickly away, she stammered, "I ... I suppose I have always admired the name."

"Lizzy, Emily tells me you wish me to look over Sir Edward's colt at Tillyard Lodge?" said Wilhelm.

"Yes, sir, if you do not mind."

"Oh, it is no trouble, I assure you."

Lizzy stood and began pacing nervously. "Rupert paid a visit."

Emily gasped. Wilhelm immediately came to her side. "The baby's father?"

She nodded. "Indeed, *the* Rupert Haworth. He still lives in London, apparently."

"When was he here, Lizzy?" said Emily.

"Last week." She shook her head in disgust. "I watched him swagger along the path toward the conservatory ... puffing his cigar. I thought he had come to take the baby, but I soon learned he did not know Lavenia was with child—he did not know he had a son."

Emily lifted the infant from Lizzy and held him to her shoulder. Shaking her head, she whispered, "Go on Lizzy."

"He said that he had come to visit Lavenia's grave. Oh, I had to tell him, Edward was his son, Emily. What was I to do? Then, beyond belief, a frumpy harlot of a woman entered unannounced. Glancing at the boys, Lizzy covered her mouth. "Oh, forgive the cursing, please."

Wilhelm gestured with his hand that it was no worry. "Young men, I do say, it is time to go scrub your hands and prepare for lunch."

"Yes, sir." The boys left the room.

Lizzy shook her head. "The woman, whom he called Charlotte, stood defiantly by his side. God Almighty, Em, I cringed. The devil urged me to let him go and not say a word about his son, but I had to tell him."

"Was he stunned, Lizzy?"

"Yes, I think so. Oh, how disgusting a situation. I pleaded for him to leave Neatham Park and never return. The baby was wailing, I was pleading—in his heart, Rupert knew. He knew Em. He felt shame. I read it in his eyes, for they softened. He vowed to never return to Neatham Park, and I believe him."

"Perhaps," said Wilhelm. He glanced at Nan. They both seemed to have known better.

* * *

Over dinner that evening, Wilhelm remarked repeatedly at how delicious the fish was. Charles and Stuart beamed.

"We must fish together next time, Father," said Charles. "It was easy enough."

"I pointed to where they were in the pond, Father," said Stuart sneaking a peek at his brother.

"Yes, yes, that is true, Father." Charles nodded wryly. "Without Stuart, I surely would not have known where to drop the hook."

Emily smiled at the boys. "I suppose you two are anxious to be leaving for London?"

Nan set her spoon aside. "Yes, I will return with you. I left the townhouse half done."

"Very well, Nan," said Emily.

Charles glanced at Lizzy, his face downcast. "Well, I'm not very anxious to return to London, ma'am. But I do miss my dogs, cats, and fish very much."

She put her arms his little shoulders. "Indeed you must, Charles. Next time we shall just bring them here. They shall never be left behind again."

"Oh, it has only been a month, Lizzy." Wilhelm laughed good-naturedly.

"To the poor little creatures without their loved ones, I would suppose it would feel like an eternity."

Stuart's face reddened. "Oh, indeed, my poor dog, Ripper. Do you suppose cook put the broom to her, Father?"

"I think not, Stuart." He hemmed. "No, I would rather suppose Ripper has been properly tied."

"And what are you do with Holly, Lizzy?" said Emily.

"I haven't given it much thought, Em."

"I beg your pardon?" said Wilhelm. "Is there something wrong?"

"No, Wil," said Emily, "but eventually Holly must be returned to her owner."

Lizzy nodded with a sigh. "She rightfully belongs to Sir Edward."

Slicing into her fillet, Emily returned, "I would not be in any great hurry to send her back, Lizzy. Wait until Dr North comes to retrieve her."

She nodded. "That sounds the best of plans, Em, but I rather suppose Lady Beatrice would relish doing that herself."

"I would then claim Holly as my own, Lizzy, and not let her go."

Lizzy's face tightened. "Depend upon it, Sister."

* * *

Later that evening after everyone had gone to bed, Lizzy and Emily sat up lounging in front of a quiet little fire. The windows were up, and a lovely summer jasmine breeze wafted about the room. The drapes moved in soft rhythm, the house was quiet, Holly lay stretched on the sofa; now and again a bark escaped her dreams.

"Sir Edward wrote to me, Emily."

"Really, love?" She set down her sherry. "And what did he write?"

Lizzy handed her his letter. "You may read it for yourself, Em."

She read the letter, folded it and handed it back. "So early in the marriage and already he is apologising for her."

"That is his nature, all goodness, all kindness," she sighed deeply.

"I suppose." Yawning, Emily covered her mouth. "And you wrote back to him?"

"Oh, yes. I told him about dearest Uncle's passing, poor Lavenia's death, the baby's health, and Holly finding her way home. I told him I would keep her until he returned to Tillyard Lodge."

"Oh, dear me, such news, such bad news to be sure—well, he had to be told. And telling him of Holly finding her way home will surely make him feel less sad. Perhaps he will just leave Holly here."

"Oh, if only Lady Beatrice does not make trouble."

"She has a husband now, Lizzy. I doubt if she would even want her back. I would imagine she has more on her mind than the worry of a hound."

"Indeed, but Sir Edward worried about her, did he not?"

Emily pressed her hand with a smile. "Yes, but then he has always thought highly of you, Lizzy."

"I must write to him soon, Em."

"About what?"

"Phoebe. It is time the foal is weaned."

"But surely you do not need his permission."

"I would feel better, Em. He has not mentioned one thing about the colt."

"Well," she contemplated, "perhaps we should ask Wilhelm."

"Indeed, Em. Tomorrow morning we shall ride over to Tillyard Lodge. Wilhelm can judge for himself."

* * *

Lizzy lay awake, even before the cock crowed that following morning. Touching her heart, she felt the steady flow in her veins. Inhaling deeply, she let a tear slide down her cheek. "Melancholy is the word at the moment."

Hearing the household stir, she sat up. Her window was open, a cool fresh breeze drifted about the room. She pushed the covers back and sat up, dangling her feet over the side, and rubbed her eyes awake. "I suppose I must dress and join everyone for breakfast."

Entering the morning room, Lizzy found everyone sitting about. Looking a little astounded at the early morning risers, she apologised, "Forgive me, have you all been waiting for me?"

The sideboard was empty, save a hot pot of coffee being poured into the urn by Helen.

"No, my dear, but we did take the liberty of having breakfast served a wee bit early. Mary was just on her way to wake you," said Emily.

Wilhelm hemmed. "I would like to make a suggestion ... we should take my carriage to Tillyard. The boys could ride atop the box, and that should make everyone happy."

"Oh, that sounds the best of plans, sir," said Lizzy.

When they arrived at Tillyard Lodge, Phoebe and her foal greeted them by running alongside the pasture fence. Just as they reached the carriage-porch, Mr Johnson stepped out onto the last step. "Oh, good morning, Miss Doddridge, Professor Meir." Pausing for a moment, he corrected himself, "Oh, yes, indeed, and Mrs Meir, you are all very welcome."

"Mr Johnson, we have come to look in on the foal," said Wilhelm.

"Indeed, sir." He glanced down. "Ah, please be patient, won't you? I am the only servant left at Tillyard."

"What? Why, what has happened to them, Mr Johnson?" asked Lizzy as she hurried to his side.

"Lady Beatrice dismissed them yesterday ... wants it shut up. I am to remain until ..." he shrugged, "until they return, I suppose."

"Oh, how dreadful, Mr Johnson," said Lizzy, her face saddened.

Professor Meir took Emily's hand. "Come along, dear. Not to worry Mr Johnson, we'll see to the foal ourselves."

While Wilhelm and Emily stood at the paddock gate, Lizzy led Phoebe and her foal into the arena. "She is a great mother. Wilhelm, there is an old-fashioned way of weaning, and I have been reading up on such matters, sir. I've read it is a far more compassionate way to separate baby from its mother. That is if you give your permission."

"Is that so? Well, then, I must hear of it. Do go on."

"Well, sir, first of all, I would not suddenly separate Phoebe from her foal. It seems to me altogether too sorrowful. You know how she grieves and how the foal becomes ever so uneasy, whinnying so for its mother."

"What do you suggest? said Emily.

Lizzy ran her hand down Phoebe's neck. "Within two months the mother's milk will be gone, and she will quite naturally wean her foal by herself. Patience, it will take a little patience. That is all. That is the old-fashioned way, apparently."

"Yes, that is one way," said Wilhelm nodding. "We have become so busy anymore, so impatient." He glanced toward the Great House. "But what of Sir Edward?"

"Oh, Mr Johnson whispered to me that he expects the Master to stay in London upon his return from the Continent. So, when he finally does come to Tillyard, he will find a healthy and happy colt old enough to train."

"And what will he find in you, Lizzy?" said Emily, gently pressing her sister's hand.

"Oh, I shan't flatter myself that he shall find anything in me at all. His life is now all research and cures. I hardly think he would give me a passing fancy." She smiled up at her sweet-faced sister and Wilhelm's gentlemanly manner. "You must be off for London in the morning. You must not give me a care. I will have the foal to wean, the baby Edward to care for, Holly ... ."

"I know you shall be very busy. I would not leave you if I felt you were abandoned. I do wish you would come to London though. Stay with Nan at the townhouse, but I know your heart is here."

"Indeed, some day I shall, but for now, I have much to do."

Chapter 9 – Chaos at Tillyard Lodge

The following day, everyone settled into the Meir carriage for their long ride to London. Nan had squeezed in between Emily and Wilhelm, nudging them with her cane. Stuart begged to sit on the box atop.

Charles rolled his eyes. "Oh, please Father, let him sit atop." He waved to Lizzy.

Giggling, she watched as their carriage twisted and turned about the gravel pathway and onto the road toward London. Stuart's little hand could still be seen waving as they disappeared into the woods.

Baby Edward began to fuss. "Very well, young man, it is nap time for you."

Mr Maxwell stood in the vestibule. "Miss Elizabeth, do you still wish the carriage readied for tomorrow's visit to Tillyard Lodge?"

"Indeed, Mr Maxwell."

The ageing butler held an unusual look—one of apprehension.

"Maxwell, what troubles you?"

"Well, miss," he paused, "there is no trouble *here*. Well, allow me to take it upon myself to inform you that there has been a great deal of re-doing at the Lodge. Shall I have the footman Watson, accompany you?"

"Watson?" She looked puzzled. "Whatever for?"

"Excuse me, Miss Elizabeth," said the grandfatherly butler, "but the comings and goings at the Lodge have me concerned."

Lizzy thought for a moment. "We were just there yesterday, Mr Maxwell. Everything seemed in order, except Mr Johnson lamented being alone."

"Very good, miss, I shall not mention it again."

"Oh, feel very free to mention anything you wish, Mr Maxwell. I find your concern comforting. I am alone now with the baby and all. No, I wish it of you to advise me of anything."

He half-bowed. "Indeed, Miss Elizabeth, I thought as much. Now, I must insist that Mr Watson accompany you."

"Very well, Mr Maxwell, very well." She studied his worried face thinking perhaps he thought the foal to be too much for her to handle alone.

The next morning Lizzy climbed into the one horse gig alongside Mr Watson. Holly snuggled in at their feet. Nearing the lodge, she noticed Phoebe and the foal were nowhere in sight.

"I am quite excited to use my experiment on the mare, Mr Watson. Indeed, no more whinnying in desperate fashion; the foal will not feel abandoned. Nor, I hope, will either injure themselves in the bargain."

"Indeed, Miss Elizabeth. I've thought the same all along. When a mare is separated from her foal, she has needless fits of despair, and for what? Just another *hurry along* if you ask me."

Now at a full stop, he helped Lizzy from the gig. "I quite agree, Mr Watson." She surveyed the area. "I suppose you may just pull the gig around back. It looks as if no one is home."

"Yes, Miss Elizabeth, I'll see to it."

"Mr Maxwell said there was a great deal of *re-doing*." She glanced around. "I wonder what he could mean, for I see nothing unusual."

"I have no idea, Miss Elizabeth."

"Well, I suppose Lady Beatrice has her plans." She tightened her scarf, tugged at her gloves and went searching for the mare.

Phoebe was a great chestnut, broad-eyed and silky. A white blaze ran from her forelock to the tip of her velvet nose. Her well-formed, suckling colt, stood very close to her side. The mare's nostrils flared, her ears pricked as Lizzy opened the half-door and walked in.

Lizzy scolded Holly, "Girl, you must stay out of the stall. Phoebe is very protective of her baby."

However, Holly thought it a game to nip at the horse's hooves.

"Very well, if you will not behave, it's the grooms' quarters for you." She led Holly into the harness-rooms finding them dark and dank. Fearful she might gnaw on the bridles and leather-work, she searched for another room. Opening one door, she leaned in and gaped. Spider webs hung in every crevice, the one lone window was opaque for dirt. Glancing around, she gawked. "Dear me, why would anyone have stored the silver and these priceless oil paintings in here? It is much too damp."

Just then she heard a carriage approach and hurried to the window, squinting through the smudged dirt. It was Lady Beatrice. Her heart thumped in her chest. "Sir Edward should be right behind her." She smiled in anticipatory wonder at seeing him again, but her smile soon faded. "She is alone. He must have decided to remain in London." Holly growled. "Shush, girl. I do not want her to find us, especially you."

Just then another carriage approached—a fine exquisite one. The four geldings pulling it were well-matched and magnificent. The groom was attired in the finest day wear, inside sat a gentleman, but it was not Sir Edward.

Lizzy frowned. "Dear me, I should wonder who *he* is."

Wonder upon wonder, when who should step out of the carriage full of self-importance and showy splendour, but Rupert Haworth. "I don't believe my eyes. What is he doing here?"

Haworth began walking toward the stables, and Lizzy hurriedly hid in a small closet, holding Holly's muzzle tight. She heard the squeaky stable door open and close. Peeking through a crack in the door, she watched Haworth go directly to the room where the silver and the oils were stored.

Holly growled. "Shush, girl," scolded Lizzy. "Shush, we mustn't be found."

Suddenly the stable door opened and Lady Beatrice entered. "Rupert, you silly fool, come away this instant! The silver and paintings are safe just where they are. No one will find them. How many times must I tell you? Do come this instant." She glanced out the window impatiently. "We must not be caught here, together."

Haworth came out of the room carrying a silver bowl, brushing spider webs from his hair. "I don't like this place one bit, *Lady* Beatrice. What if that buffoon of a husband of yours stumbles upon it?"

Lizzy's jaw dropped. *Buffoon?*

"He never comes near here, buckle head, so never mind."

"Yeah, well servants are crawling all over the place."

"They have all been let go. There is only Johnson now, and he's too old to even find his privates."

"All the same, I'm not havin' any of it. I want my share now and be done with it."

"You'll be done when I say so, now put that silver back."

He sneered. "You been uppity ever since you came back from your little honeymoonin.' No need talking to me like I were a dog. I ain't no dog, and you better mind your mouth." He pulled a cigar from his vest and defiantly stuck it in his mouth. "Gaming ain't your strong suit, Lady High and Mighty, and from now on, you ain't not gambling a penny more of my share. If I don't get what you owe me within the week, I'm going to Papa." He grabbed her throat. "He'll be so delighted to hear that his one and only dearest little girl is up to her neck in debt. Indeed, sneakin' silver, fine wines, paintings and such from her unsuspecting husband's mansion and gambling with the proceeds. He'll be very impressed."

Her face turned white, breaking free, she spit in his face. "You better not even step one foot into my father's house, or I'll have you arrested. Don't forget I know you and I know your plans to steal your bastard son for ransom."

His face twisted into purple-red scorn. Clenching his fist, he reached for her. "He's no bastard ... ."

She stood her ground. "Don't even think about touching me again you filthy louse. I've written a letter to my father, if I disappear you'll be the first arrested. It's all there, how you ransacked the Lodge, your plans to steal the baby. I'll gamble what and when I please. Now, get out! You'll not get another penny from me!"

He calmly set the silver bowl on the rough-hewn table. Wiping his forehead on his sleeve, he took in a deep breath. "Well, now, no need for getting all wily, Lady Bea. No need. I'll go now. Indeed, gamble what you want." He straightened his shoulders and exhaled heavily. "I have my plans, you have yours. That's simple enough. Just pay me what you owe me and be done with it."

She held the door open. "Get out."

Lizzy closed her eyes in disbelief. She held tight to Holly's muzzle whispering, "Good girl." *Oh, what about Mr Watson? What if he should be discovered?*

The door closed. Lizzy heard voices in the stable, but they soon dissipated. Slowly she opened the door. "Shush now, girl."

Then suddenly the door swung open, Lizzy stepped back, holding her breath.

"Oh, Miss Lizzy," said Watson, "I found you."

"Oh, indeed," she exhaled deeply, "we must leave, now."

"What's wrong, miss? Did I frighten you?"

Lizzy put her finger to her lips. "We must be very quiet, Watson," she whispered. There is mayhem at every turn." She tiptoed to the window and peeked out. "Dear me, Mr Haworth has left."

Watson peeked over her shoulder. "I see nothing, miss."

"We must leave at once, Mr Watson, that scoundrel, Haworth, may be heading to Neatham to steal baby Edward."

"What? Steal the child?"

They ran to the waiting gig. Flicking the whip to the horse's rump, they were at a steady gallop in an instant. Lizzy held onto her hat, Holly had squirmed in between the two. "I will have Maxwell take baby Edward to London to stay with Professor Meir and Emily," said Lizzy squinting in the wind.

"Indeed, Miss Lizzy, that's the best plan."

"Then we must hurry back to the Lodge." She dropped her head in her hands and cried, "Oh, I have a feeling poor Mr Johnson is in danger. Lady Beatrice just may have done him harm."

"Miss Elizabeth, Johnson, is my cousin. Is Lady Beatrice involved in this mayhem you spoke about?"

"I am afraid so, Watson."

She explained the evil dealings she overheard in the stables between Haworth and Lady Beatrice.

Watson shook his head. "Indeed, my cousin just may be in great danger."

As they pulled under the carriage-porch at Neatham, Lizzy jumped from the gig. "Watson, have the carriage readied. I will find Maxwell and have him take Edward to London. We'll then return to the Lodge and secure Johnson."

She ran into the servants' quarters shouting for Maxwell.

Helen hurried out. "Oh, Miss Lizzy, he is in the dining room."

Lizzy found him polishing the silver. "Mr Maxwell, make ready. You are going to London with the baby. Hurry now, I have not the time to explain."

"Oh, indeed, Miss Lizzy. Oh, indeed." He dropped his cloth and hurried to his room.

"Helen, come with me. Pack everything of Edward's, everything. Make haste!"

When Lizzy ran into the nursery to fetch the baby, he was gone. "Where is he, Helen?"

"Where is he?" She pushed past her and stopped, staring into the empty bassinette. "Why, Mary must have taken him for a stroll in the garden."

Lizzy ran to the balcony and glanced out. "She is nowhere in sight." She dashed back down the stairs and met Mary in the hall. "Where is the baby, Mary?"

"Why, Miss Lizzy, he is taking his nap."

"Oh, God," she dropped into a chair, "he has taken him already."

Holly rushed to her side, whining.

Helen took Mary's hand. "By my life, I don't know what's happening. Who took him?"

Pulling on his waistcoat, Maxwell hurried into the room. "Miss Elizabeth, what is the trouble?"

Just then Watson entered. "I have the carriage ready." He stared at Maxwell, "Where is the baby?"

"Rupert has taken him," cried Lizzy, "and I do not know what can be done about it." She wrung her hands. "If something should happen to that child ... ."

Watson slapped his fist hard against the wall. "The rat catcher must have sneaked in and stolen him while everyone's backs were turned."

Just then Rupert Haworth strolled into the room. "Excuse me, excuse me, pray-tell, how does one steal one's own?" He spun on his heels to face Lizzy. "Edward is my son. I defy anyone claiming otherwise." He glanced at the sobbing Lizzy. "Shut up, Elizabeth. It's bad enough to have a screaming baby around, and now to have a snivelling moron is doubly unnerving."

"What have you done with my baby, you monster." Lizzy ran toward him, but Watson grabbed her.

"That's right, Watson, restrain the lady." Swiftly removing his pocket knife, he deftly flicked it open with one hand. "I just might have to protect myself ... perhaps carve a few more scars on her face." A shrill laugh escaped, "Oh, the thrill of it all."

Watson took a step. "Watch your mouth, Haworth, I'm warning you."

"Oh, you big ignorant oaf, do take a seat." He scoffed, "Put one hand on me ... ." he looked at everyone in the room, "anybody puts a hand on me, and the baby is doomed." With one quick motion of his hand, he snapped the knife shut and shoved it back into his pocket.

The room grew quiet.

"There, that's what I most enjoy about an assembly such as this, quiet all around." He glanced out the window. "My son, right this minute, is in my carriage. My dear wife, Lady Charlotte, is tending him. My accomplices are well hidden, and they carry pistols." He smiled. "Ah, all is safe, all is right, I have my son back." He took Helen by the shoulder. "And now, my fat scullery maid, you will run upstairs and pack all of his things and take them to my waiting carriage."

Helen brought her hands to her mouth, "I canno do such a thing."

"I said now!" Rupert shouted. Spittle flew about her face. "Now!"

Helen dashed away crying. "Very well, very well."

"Oh, do this, do that, quite the Master I am, wouldn't you say?" Haworth took hold of his lapels and leaned back on his heels. "Light my cigar, Watson."

Taking the candle sitting on the mantle, Watson's jaw settled into a stubborn mould. He lit Rupert's cigar and forcefully threw the candle into the fire.

"Careful, careful, my good man." Haworth inhaled, sucking up until the tip flickered red. Thick grey smoke curled up, meandering heavily about the air. He exhaled a puff of smoke into Watson's face. "Take a seat, you fat ox. I am quite done with you, for the moment." He smirked.

Watson's face turned a deeper red, his fists clenched.

"What do you want from me, Rupert" Lizzy wiped her eyes. "Name anything you want, but bring the child back into the house immediately."

"Well now, do I hear a bit of pleading in that voice of yours my dear?" He laughed.

She nodded. "You do."

Haworth glanced around the room. "Pack all the silver, all the jewellery."

"Very well, Rupert." Lizzy instructed Mary to gather it.

"No," he said, as he looked at the butler, "Maxwell will get it. Pile it all on the table. Don't forget I lived here, and if I find that you have not brought forth every bit of silver and every bit of jewellery, then dear baby Edward will be sent looking for it." He laughed. "Go now before I turn ugly."

Maxwell nodded. "Very well."

"And one more thing, Maxwell, don't forget to empty dear ol' Uncle's strongbox. It's hidden behind the Queen's portrait in his room. I'm assuming you have the key?"

He nodded. "I have the key."

"Then move on, I haven't all day." Haworth rubbed his cigar out on the heel of his boot scattering ashes and hot sparks all over Uncle's revered 16th-century Oriental rug.

Maxwell winced.

Within the hour all the household silver—candelabras, bowls, plates, drinking vessels, all of it stacked neatly on the long rectangular table in the breakfast room. Rolled in fine muslin was the family's silverware sitting in its carved mahogany chest—the name Doddridge carved on the lid, next to it sat the family cutlery box.

"There now," said Haworth fingering the silver, "my son's rightful inheritance. I shall just keep it for safekeeping." He glanced at Lizzy. "Until he reaches an age, of course."

Maxwell carefully set down a gentleman's rosewood dressing case on the table, the key next to it. "I have not opened it. Therefore I have no idea what is inside."

Haworth lit up. "Well, well, then." He took the key and gently inserted it into the well-worn keyhole and unlatched it. He picked out a dozen or so solid gold cufflinks and rolled them onto the table like dice. "Well, it seems I've hit the jackpot," he laughed. "Oh, well, not me of course, my son has." He retrieved the links and tossed them back into the case. Rummaging through the box with one finger, he smiled. "Yes indeed, vest buttons, shirt buttons, studs ..." He suddenly slammed the lid shut and locked it, depositing the key into his vest pocket. "Keep searching, Maxwell."

Haworth noticed a gold chain with a cross hanging from Lizzy's neck. "Well, well, that looks familiar." When he reached to examine it, Lizzy jerked back. "Over my dead body, Rupert, this was Lavenia's."

Holly sunk low on her haunches; hair bristled on her neck, her teeth were bared.

He backed away. "Very well, you may keep it. I shouldn't have need for religious objects." He glanced back at the hound and made motion to kick her, but thought better of the idea. "Humph, I thought I killed every last one of you mongrels."

"Leave her alone, Rupert." Lizzy's blue eyes sparkled defiantly. She held his gaze daring him to move one step closer to the dog.

Haworth shook his head, spitting bits of tobacco. "Pitiful." He turned to Maxwell. "Put dear old Uncle's strongbox next to my coat in the hall, and give me the key."

Maxwell glanced at the handful of keys on his ring. "I have no idea where Mr Doddridge kept *that* key."

"No worry," he shrugged, "I have plenty of friends who would know just how to open such a case."

"I'm sure you do, Rupert," said Lizzy with a smirk.

"I'm warning you, Elizabeth, don't press your luck with me."

Maxwell had Mary and Helen pack all the silver in trunks. Haworth's footmen hurriedly carried them to his waiting carriage.

Peeking out the window, Lizzy stood anxious. Haworth's new wife was waiting in the carriage holding the baby. She spied Edward's little patch quilt of blue and yellow. "Rupert, you have everything, now have Edward brought back into the house this very instant."

"You delight in handing out orders, don't you Elizabeth?" He tugged at his gloves and put his hat on. "Well, what need do I have with a troublesome, whiny tag-a-long."

"No need at all, Rupert."

"Indeed not."

Lizzy anxiously walked alongside him to the waiting carriage. The trunks full of silver were stacked and tied, Uncle's strong box sat on the seat across from Haworth's wife.

"Lady Charlotte," said Rupert to his wife, "do be a dear and hand over my son to Elizabeth."

"What?" she said, squinting, her weather-beaten hat sat lopsided on her frizzy, balding head. "Ruppy, ain't we gonna keep him? He's your blood, darlin'."

"Shut up and ... ."

In haste, Lizzy elbowed her way into the carriage. "I'll take the baby." She snatched the child and backed out. "Thank you, Rupert." She cradled the fussing baby. "You won't be sorry."

"Oh, I know I won't be sorry." He directed his footman to drop the baby's trunk on the ground. "You may keep him until I return." He climbed into the carriage and tapped his walking stick to the ceiling panel. "Move on."

Lizzy hurried into the house. "Maxwell, take the baby to London, to Emily. His trunk is just outside." She kissed Edward's forehead with a defiant smile. "I shall not give you up, little man, never." She glanced at Maxwell. "Hurry along now before Rupert changes his mind and comes back."

"Indeed," said Helen, "Haworth is quite the scoundrel."

"Helen, do go with Maxwell, will you?"

"Oh, indeed, Miss Lizzy."

Lizzy hugged her. "Thank you, both." She grabbed her bonnet and wrap. "I will take the gig to Tillyard Lodge. I must find Mr Johnson."

"I'm coming along."

"Thank you, Mr Watson."

She met Mary in the hall. "Mary, if Mr Haworth returns, tell him the baby became ill and I rushed him to the apothecary in the village."

"Yes, Miss Lizzy."

She and Watson climbed into the gig. Snapping the horse's rump with his whip, he shouted, "Hup, hup."

"I'll take the low road to Tillyard, miss. We need to stay off the high road—don't want to run into that scoundrel if we can help it." He shook the whip in his hand. "But this can be mighty persuasive if need be."

They arrived behind the stables to the whinnying of Phoebe. Her foal was still in his own paddock. "Oh, sorry girl, I forgot about him. Do forgive me." The anxious mare nickered as Lizzy led the foal back into the pen with her.

Suddenly the barn door opened, Lizzy and Watson backed up against the wall, now half hidden by Phoebe. They watched Lady Beatrice come out of the grooms' quarters. She held a club dangerously close to Johnson's head. "That's the last of it. Now, put the rest of the silver in my carriage and be quick about it you old toad."

"Very well, madam." He straightened. "And then, what will happen to me?"

She cackled. "Never mind, hurry along now old man before I ... ."

Lizzy and Watson watched as the ageing butler shuffled out into the stable yard with Lady Beatrice at his heals. She slammed the stable door and locked it.

"Her carriage is still there," whispered Lizzy. "She must have emptied the room of all the silver and the paintings. Well, come, let us see for ourselves."

They opened the spare harness-room door and peeked in.

Empty, just as I thought," said Lizzy. "So the thief made way. I wonder what Rupert will do when he finds she's absconded with his loot as well."

As they hurried out the back, Lizzy stopped. Sniffing the air, she grabbed Watson's sleeve. "There is a fire."

Looking toward the Great House, she spied Lady Beatrice hurrying into her carriage. Within seconds it was bouncing down the lane, dust curling up in great clouds following behind.

"I smell it too, said Watson.

"Look," Lizzy pointed, "smoke!" She ran toward the servants' entrance. Bright orange-yellow flames were wildly consuming the kitchen, the windows were cracking and shattering, black smoke billowed from the doors and chimneys.

"Mr Johnson, Johnson, where are you?" shouted Lizzy.

Flames had now spread into the pantry. The dining room would be engulfed in seconds.

"I'll check the other side of the house," said Watson, coughing through the smoke.

"Very well." Lizzy found the front entrance unlocked and ran inside. Hearing a faint cry, she and rushed down the back servants' hall until coming to the stairs. Black smoke was now pouring in from all directions. She slammed the dining room door to stave off the flames. Hearing a moan, she ran down the hall. "It's coming from up there." She dashed up the back steps and finding the livery door closed, she kicked it open. "Oh, Mr Johnson." She found the elder butler lying on the floor, his mouth gagged, his wrists tied.

"Oh, dear me, Mr Johnson, hold still." She removed the gag and cradled his head onto her lap. "Oh, sir, hold on, I will untie your wrists."

"Oh, dear me," he moaned, "I smell smoke."

"Indeed, we must hurry. She set the place afire."

Lizzy helped him up. "Come now, we must get out of here." When she opened the door, a wall of fire blasted into the room. Stumbling back, she wiped the black cinders from her face. Stunned she stood motionless. Johnson kicked the door closed. Pushing her toward the window, he shouted, "Jump!"

She hesitated, "You first, Johnson."

"Jump before it's too late, miss."

Lizzy grabbed his frail little arm and pulled him to the window. The room was fast filling with smoke. "Hurry now, Johnson, climb out onto the roof. I'll be right behind you."

The old butler creaked and groaned and finally slid from the window out onto the roof. He turned back and pulled Lizzy out. The fire suddenly blasted into the room forcing them to the edge of the roof. The back of Lizzy's dress was afire, her thick black hair was smouldering.

A voice from down below shouted, "This way!" It was Sir Edward standing on his carriage roof. "Jump, Elizabeth!"

"Oh, God, sir," she felt the hot red heat singe her skin, "I can't."

Johnson wrapped his arms around her and stepped off the roof.

* * *

Lizzy jolted awake, feeling wetness to her lips. She tried to sit up, but was pressed back. "No, you must not move, Miss Elizabeth," said Sir Edward.

"What?" She glanced around the room, her head felt dizzy, she closed her eyes. "Sir Edward, is that you?"

"Do not excite yourself, Miss Elizabeth," he said soothingly, "you must rest."

"Why must I rest?" Becoming agitated, she again tried to sit up. "Where is the baby? What has happened to the baby?"

Sir Edward pressed her hand. "Do calm yourself Miss Elizabeth, the child is with Emily and Wilhelm. He is doing very well, I assure you."

She settled back with a sigh. "Oh, that is very good, very good, indeed." Glancing down at her strange raiment, the room, and the stark white walls, she frowned. "Is this a hospital?"

He nodded. "The very same one I brought you to last year. I might add, in the very same carriage ... though the roof is a little damaged." He gently tweaked her nose. "You took another fall."

"Then I am in London, sir?" she asked in a whisper, searching his face. She tenderly ran her fingers over his soft, tanned skin, the crinkly lines about his soft brown eyes; *I have missed you terribly.* Her eyes pooled with tears, she thought of his wife and Rupert. "Oh, Sir Edward, there is something dreadful I must tell you."

He put his finger to her lips. "There is no need."

Her eyes flashed as she again she tried to sit up. "Oh, but there is a need, sir, your very life is in danger." She wept. "I could not bear it if you were ..."

He put his arms around her and gently hugged her. "No need to worry, Eliza. My life is now out of danger because of you." He dabbed her eyes. "Look here, you see, I am using my handkerchief rather than some old pair of knickers—that should make you laugh."

She giggled. "Oh, indeed, sir." She smiled. "You called me Eliza?" Suddenly an odd expression spread across her face when she reached behind her head to fondle her lustrous thick hair, but she found only a handful of short cropped curls.

"I had to cut it, Eliza. The fire singed most of it. I had to cut your frock off as well." He shook his head. "The roof collapsed, had you not jumped you would have perished within seconds."

She glanced at her left arm wrapped in white cloth. "Is it singed as well? I can hardly move it." She winched. "Oh, dear Mr Johnson, he saved my life."

"You saved his life, Eliza."

She looked incredulous. "But how can that be? He pulled me from the roof."

"You broke his fall, my dear."

She closed her eyes. "I cannot remember that so very well, Sir Edward."

"From now on you shall call me Edward." He affectionately tweaked her nose.

Her face glowed. "Indeed, sir."

The door opened, and Emily and Wilhelm entered. Nan, struggling on her cane, made way to the head of the bed. Wilhelm, with hat in hand, nodded. Emily kissed her forehead.

"It's about time you woke up," said Nan shaking her head, "been waiting the whole day long."

"Can you find it in your heart to forgive me, Nan?" she jested.

Emily took her hand. "It is not a thing to joke about, Lizzy. You gave us all quite a fright."

"Well, I hope to never repeat it, Sister." She glanced at Nan. "You are right Nan, the flames of hell are very hot, indeed."

"Indeed, much too warm," she said with a smirk. "But then, *I'll* never see the day."

Sir Edward hemmed. "Well, I must be going."

Lizzy grabbed his hand. "Oh, sir, surely I am not well enough for you to leave." She pouted. "Edward, surely you will not leave me."

"I must." He pressed her hand. "I promise to return to you within the month."

Her jaw dropped. "Within the month? Surely you jest, Edward?"

"Very well, give me two weeks." He smiled down at her. "Much in my life needs sorting out. It should have been taken care of by now, but I could not leave your side." He kissed her hand.

"Oh, very well then, Edward, if you must go, I will understand."

Emily and Wilhelm removed to the window, giving them privacy. Nan shuffled from the room.

Edward lowered his voice. "Two weeks at the most. You shall be discharged within the week, that is, if you listen to the doctors and do as I have instructed."

"I will, Edward," she said in a whisper, "I promise."

"I will next see you at Neatham Park."

"Oh, Edward ... ." Lizzy motioned for him to come closer. "I must tell you something before you leave me."

"Oh, indeed." He bent over very close so as to listen.

She placed her hand around his neck and kissed his mouth. "I love you, Edward."

* * *

Lizzy's left arm was broken and burned, but not severely. With a good bit of care, it would mend. However, she would always carry the scars.

Now resettled at Neatham Park, Lizzy walked slowly toward her revered glass atrium. "Edward has not seen it yet, Nan. He will be astounded, for I have replicated every detail to a tee. Even the flowers are the very same."

"Oh, I'm sure there are a few things you have forgotten, you always do," she teased.

Still giggling from Nan's humour, Lizzy spied Mr Johnson, "Oh, there you are, Johnson, I need your assistance with baby Edward's bassinette."

"Indeed, Miss Elizabeth," said the elder gentleman, dressed in his immaculate white shirt, black waistcoat, and

Uncle's gold cufflinks, a gift from her. Though now slower, his position at Neatham Park was permanent.

Lizzy watched as he slowly carried the baby's bed and sat it in the conservatory.

"Yes, that is it exactly," said Lizzy with a smile. "Remember the tub, Johnson? Remember when I bathed Holly as a pup?" She looked up. "Yes, you placed it right here, exactly where the bassinette is now placed."

"Oh, indeed I do, miss," he chuckled. "What a memory."

"You know Johnson, you don't have to continue to serve. Your place here should be one of relaxation and ease."

"That's right, we've earned our keep. Now come, Johnson, walk with me in the garden," said Nan. "Hurry along now." She poked him with her cane.

He nodded with a smile. "It seems I am surrounded by women I must obey."

"Well, after all," said Nan gesturing toward Watson with her cane, "this young man needs a butler's position, if you must know."

Watson nodded with a smile.

"And you'll do very well," said Lizzy. "Very well, indeed."

* * *

The air was warm, the sun rested at its highest peak in the late August sky. Lizzy glanced down at baby Edward while he slept. Her favourite chair was situated in the conservatory, the baby's black walnut bassinette swung slowly at her side. Holly lay curled about the cool black soil of flowers; ivy twisted and curled up the trellised walls. Lizzy dozed off in the noon heat, a letter from Sir Edward dangled from her hand.

Suddenly Holly was up. Her entire body wagged in grand fashion. Lizzy sat up, "What's wrong, girl?" Turning, she found Sir Edward standing in awe of the atrium. "I, I thought all of this was destroyed in the fire, Eliza." He took her hand. "What have you done?"

With her good hand, she took his arm and snuggled close to him. "When Lady Beatrice said it was to be torn down, I had the Millers' from Alton save every piece of it. While you were on honeymoon, I had them reassembled it here ... its exact replica."

"And my roses ... you saved them as well?" He looked dumbfounded. "Why, I had no idea your feelings were so deep.

Elizabeth, I am truly ashamed." He dropped his head. "I neglected you so. Forgive me."

Snuggling closer, she whispered, "Well, sir, you will have the rest of your life to make it up."

He pulled away from her and walked a few short steps. Holding his hat in his hand, he turned his back to her. "I am sorry, but I must return to London."

"Return to London, sir? But you just got here."

He turned and faced her, his features ashen and pained. "Elizabeth, I behaved with a little more sentimentality than I should have in the hospital. I couldn't help myself. You are a very striking creature. We shall remain friends, forever."

Lizzy's face wrinkled in confusion, her mouth went dry; her heart stopped beating. "Friends?"

"Elizabeth, while consulting my attorney, I have been informed that while Beatrice is in prison, a divorce is impossible." His face turned to stone. "The fact of the matter is, she will be there for the rest of her life." He pursed his lips. "All I have left of my life now is my work. Good-bye, Eliza."

"But Edward, it is just good-bye then?"

"You are young and beautiful. You deserve a full life with a man of worth and have many children ... of your own."

"But you are a man of worth, sir, I adore you."

"But not a free one, Eliza." He stiffened. "I will not sully your fine reputation by remaining a second longer in your company. Good night."

Lizzy stood in the atrium, tears streamed freely down her cheeks as she watched him leave. Sobbing, she buried her head in her hands. "A fine reputation for a spinster ... and I care nothing for it."

Chapter 10 – The Spinster Lizzy

Twenty years have passed, and Lizzy has remained a spinster tending her revered roses and raising Edward as her own. Her sister, Emily still happily married also raised Wilhelm's two boys as her own, Charles and Stuart.

Edward Lavenia Doddridge graduated from Oxford, a fine young gentleman. Charles and Stuart Meir were Edward's best friends, and the cousins remained close.

To celebrate Edward's graduation, the three young men stopped in at the Red Lily for a pint. It was a quaint little pub just a little distance from the Doddridge Townhouse, London.

Patting Edward on the back, Charles beamed. "Very well done, Dr Edward Doddridge, Botanist, indeed. I am very proud of you, sir."

"Indeed, Cousin," said Edward, "but it is I who should pat you both on the back. Without your diligent insistence, I would never have made it through Oxford. Look at you Charles, a doctor of medicine and you, Stuart, a veterinarian."

Stuart nodded humbly as he sipped his ale. "Nonsense, my good man, you were destined to a life of science all your life. So, ol' chap what are your plans now? Where do you think you'll do your research?"

"America," Edward sat down his tankard, "where there is land aplenty. I should like to have my own vast garden of roses."

"And so you shall," said Charles with a huge grin. "New York, perhaps? I would love to holiday in New York."

"I am thinking of New Jersey, actually."

"And Aunt Lizzy?"

"Oh, she will come with me of course. She is my mother, after all."

"Will Neatham Park remain in the family?" asked Stuart. "I so love the place, Eddie."

"Oh, I suppose, but that is up to our mothers—they are such sentimentalists. As you know, I was born there, to my first mother, Lavenia." He sighed deeply. "She is buried there."

Charles nodded. "Indeed, Eddie. Taking the Doddridge name and calling Aunt Lizzy *Mother* seems so right and natural to us, but to some, it must be confusing."

Stuart nodded. "And what about your father, Rupert Haworth, what about him, Edward?"

"Well, I shan't visit him again, depend upon it. Prison is a very depressing place. Besides, I do not for a second believe he has learned his lesson very well."

"No, I suppose he never will," agreed Charles.

"He constantly asks for money. I think he still gambles it away without regard. If we stay in England, I am sure when he gets out he'll find us and repeat his demands."

Stuart ordered another pint. "I heard Sir Edward's wife died."

Edward stiffened. "When?"

"Just a few days ago," Stuart shrugged. "At the hands of a few prisoners, so I have been told."

Charles shuddered. "How gruesome, but from what Father has told me, Lady Beatrice was a wicked dealer from the very beginning ... probably got caught up in her own web."

Edward sighed deeply. "After all these years Sir Edward is finally free. I do not think he ever forgot my mother."

"No, I suppose not, but saddled with such a wife, *Lady* Beatrice, indeed." Stuart shook his head, "I could hardly blame the old chap for being a recluse. I wonder what he'll do now?"

"I do not know," said Edward. "Mother never speaks about him but to admire the gentleman's fine moral fibre and dedication to his work."

"Indeed," said Charles, "I heard Sir Edward recently met with Dr Gaffky ..."

"The prominent German scientist?"

Charles nodded. "The very one. They say he's very close to identifying the cause of typhoid. As you know, that is my field of speciality. I am truly fortunate to have an affiliation with Sir Edward. And you, Cousin, you carry his very name."

Edward nodded. "Indeed, he has been a good friend and counsellor through the years sponsoring me at Oxford, his alma mater. Indeed, a fine gentleman. He has always been very happy that I so adore flowers, particularly his roses. He wanted to attend my graduation, but he shuns the crowds, you know. Now and again he visits with Her Majesty."

"I suppose they commensurate with one another."

"Well, she at least has Mr Brown."

"So I have heard." Edward stood. "Well, my dear chaps, I must be going. Mother is expecting me at six."

"All right, then, Eddie. Stuart and I are coming for Sunday dinner. Emily and Father are to be there as well. See you then, ol' boy."

* * *

Edward arrived at the Doddridge Townhouse and went directly to his room to change for dinner. When he came down in search of his mother, he found Mr Watson at the foot of the stairs.

"Beg pardon, Master Edward, but your mother is lying down. Apparently, she has taken a fever."

"Oh? Well, then I shall see for myself." He knocked lightly at her door before entering.

"Come," she replied with a raspy voice.

He peeked around the door and found her bundled under at least three quilts. "Oh, dearest Mother," he said coming to her bedside, "I am sorry to hear you are unwell." He felt her brow.

"Oh, it is nothing, Edward, a slight cold or something. I must have caught a chill at your graduation ceremonies. The weather, you know, changes so quickly anymore. It won't be the first cold I've suffered through."

He glanced around the room. "Are you warm enough, Mother?" He grabbed another quilt and gently spread it over her. "There now, that should do."

"Yes, that feels very good, dear. Now, tell me, how were your cousins?" Her voice weakened.

"Oh, we had a pint and discussed medicine. There is a prominent German, a Dr Gaffky, who is close to discovering the reason for the typhoid, Mother. Of course, Charles is very excited about it." He felt her brow again and frowned. "Mother, you are very warm. I think I shall call Charles and have him see you."

"Oh, nonsense, Edward, you must not disturb the dear boy. It is only a cold, I shall live."

"Well," he walked to the hearth and dropped two more logs onto the fire, "I shall have Mary bring up some broth and toast with marmalade then."

She smiled. "Indeed, you sound like Nan, bless her."

He poked the logs. "Indeed, I miss her, Mother."

"She was like a mother to me." Lizzy's eyes moistened. She sneezed and brought her covers to her neck, shivering. "Well, I think I shall just rest my eyes, they are burning."

Edward felt her brow again. "I'll have cook hurry with your broth, Mother." Backing away, he remained in the open doorway looking back at her. *I wonder if I should just have Charles look in on her. What's the harm? She might possibly scold me, but ... well, I'd rather be safe.*

On his way to the kitchen, he thought of their earlier conversation regarding the typhoid. *Perhaps I am just overreacting. Mother is sound and healthy as a horse. She rarely gets sick with cold. But then again ...*

Edward took the tray up to his mother's room entering without knocking. She was asleep with her covers still to her chin. The room was very warm, a nice fire crackled in the hearth. Setting the tray at the foot of her bed, he touched her brow with the back of his hand. "Dear, you are much too warm."

He sat at her desk and wrote a hurried note to Charles explaining that Aunt Lizzy was ill with fever and needed him.

"Mr Watson, I want this note delivered to Dr Charles Meir, immediately."

"Oh, indeed, sir. Is Miss Lizzy doing worse?"

"I'm afraid so."

"I'll deliver it myself, sir."

* * *

Reading the urgent message, Charles hurriedly grabbed his bag and accompanied Watson back to the Doddridge Townhouse. Entering Lizzy's room, he found Edward holding her hand as she slept.

Edward stood. "Oh, thank God, you have come."

Charles sat his case on the nightstand. "Let me take a look."

"Thank you, Charles. Mother hasn't awoken. I brought a tray of broth, but she was sleeping so soundly ... I didn't want to wake her."

Charles touched her brow with the back of his hand. "Indeed, she is high with fever."

Lizzy's eye's fluttered open, they were red and filmy. She tried to speak, but had no voice. Her breath was hot and sour.

"There now Mother," Edward pressed her hand, "I thought it prudent to have Charles look at you."

He smiled, "Indeed, Aunt Lizzy, you are very sick. I'm not sure if it is just a cold or the influenza." He glanced at the bowl on her tray. "What if we spooned some broth into you?"

She shook her head.

"No? Well, I think a spoonful would be wise." He parted her lips with the tip of the spoon and emptied it into her mouth. Her lips were chapped and waxy.

Edward paced in front of the hearth. "Charles, what is going to happen?"

"Edward, why don't you go downstairs? I can manage here. I'm afraid all of this is too much for you. Go now, I'll be down shortly."

"Very well, Charles." Edward stood for a very long time watching his mother's face, holding her limp hand. Her eyes, now red with fever, held his gaze. She nodded with a smile as if to say *go now, I'll be fine, dear*.

Within the hour, Charles entered the library. "There you are, Eddie. Aunt Lizzy is, indeed, very sick. I will keep the night by her side. If she becomes delirious, we must remove her to the hospital ... for tests."

"Tests? You mean for the typhoid, Charles?" His face paled.

"Eddie, let us not think too far ahead of ourselves."

* * *

Lizzy's mantle clock struck four soft tinny chimes.

Charles took her limp wrist and felt for a pulse. His face tightened. "It is weak, Eddie."

Edward stood. "Oh, I know what that means." He pulled the cord for Mr Watson. "We must take Mother to the hospital."

The door opened, and Watson hurried in. "Sir?"

Edward stepped back. "But, Watson, I just this moment rang for you."

"I've been waiting at the door, sir."

"What would Mother do without you, Mr Watson?"

He nodded proudly. "The carriage is ready, sir."

"We must keep her covered and warm," said Charles.

"I will carry her," said Edward.

"Victoria, sir?"

Charles nodded. "Yes, Mr Watson, Victoria Hospital."

Edward carried Lizzy into the hospital and was immediately settled into a frigid, white, sparsely furnished room in the quarantine section. He glanced around. "Charles, it is far too cold in this room. We can't possibly leave her here."

"Eddie, lay her on the bed. The coolness will feel very good to her."

He hesitated. "Well, I'm not so sure."

"Go ahead now, Eddie, lay her down. She'll be far more comfortable not bundled so in your arms."

The nurses scurried about the room carrying trays, tiny medicine bottles, and towels.

"Very well, Charles."

The nurses fluffed up the stark white pillows as he gently lay her on the bed. "There you are, my dear." He kissed her cheek.

Charles sighed deeply. "Come away, ol' chap, let them do their work. I'll be with her."

Edward looked around the room with doubt. "No, I shall remain."

"They do not want you here, Eddie. That is why there are no chairs. Come along now. There is a small chapel just down the hall."

"A chapel, for what?" He grabbed Charles's arm. Tears sprung to his eyes. "Is Mother going to ... ?"

"No, Edward, you have my word."

"Your word?" He shook his head. "How could you possibly give your word?"

* * *

Emily, Wilhelm, and Stuart hurried into the hospital. They found Edward in the waiting room, his head resting in his hands.

"Oh, God, Edward," said Emily, "how is she?"

He shook his head, "Not very well, Aunt Emily."

"Is Charles with her?" said Wilhelm.

He nodded, his voice hoarse, "All night." He looked up, his eyes bloodshot, his hair tousled, his face with stubble. "I do not know what to say."

Emily took his hand. "Say nothing, dearest. Just know that we are with you."

Stuart put his arm around him. "Indeed, Eddie, we are with you."

The town clock struck eight. Edward stood, yawned and stretched. Emily and Wilhelm huddled close, holding hands. Stuart stood at the window; his springy bright red hair glowed in the bright morning sun.

Lizzy opened her eyes. Lifting her head from the pillow, she felt the room swirl. *Dear me, how horrid I feel.* She closed her eyes. *I'm burning with fever, perhaps I shall die today.*

She heard the door open, felt a cool hand touch her brow, there was that familiar lavender scent. She squinted up at the man bending over her.

"Eliza, dearest," he whispered, "you do not have the typhoid."

She tried to focus, rubbing her eyes awake. "Edward, how very nice to see you."

He lovingly smoothed away the matted hair from her face. "Did you hear what I said, Eliza? You do not have the typhoid."

"Yes, I heard you," she said with a deep sigh. "So, I am going to live after all?"

"Indeed," he nodded, "but you are still very sick with the influenza."

He took up her arm that had been burned years ago. "Still a few scars, but remarkable skin, Eliza, you healed beautifully."

"The Lodge fire was so long ago, Edward."

He took her chin examining her face. "And clearly, not one scar from first our meeting in London—do you remember, dear?"

She nodded a faint smile. "Oh, how well I remember the day ... ." Suddenly she lurched, gagged, and spit up. "Oh, God, not again."

Grabbing a towel, he laughed as he tenderly dabbed her chin. Holding it up, he laughed. "And mind, no knickers this time."

Though very weak, she took his hand, her brow beaded with perspiration, her eyes still red, but she managed a giggle. "I have missed you terribly, Edward."

"Beatrice is dead, Eliza."

"I know."

He took her in his arms, cradling her limp, sick body and buried his head in her neck. "Oh, how I have missed you, my dearest sweetest Eliza. Will you marry me?"

Just then Edward entered. When he saw his mother limp in the arms of Sir Edward, he thought the worst of it. "Oh, no, no, this cannot be!"

Hearing Edward's anguish, Emily, Wilhelm, and Stuart pushed into the room. Stuart put his arms around his brother.

Sir Edward turned to them with a smile, still holding Lizzy in his arms. "She does not have the typhoid."

A cry escaped Emily as she hurried to her sister's side.

"Oh, Sir Edward," said Eddie wiping his tears, "thank God." He took Lizzy's hand. "Mother, you gave me such a fright. I informed Sir Edward of your condition very early this morning, and he immediately rushed to your side—still wearing his sleeping gown and cap, I might add."

Wilhelm hemmed. "Indeed, Lizzy, he tested you in his own lab. We watched him dash away and then return this morning—he rushed past us all as he hurried into your room."

"Indeed," said Emily kissing her sister's hand, "we could not wait a moment longer to know."

Stuart sniffed the air and wrinkled his nose. "Dr North, sir, what is that on the front of your white lab coat, pray tell?"

Other Great Novels by this Author

Winthrope – *Tragedy to Triumph*
The Arrangement – *Love Prevails*
Bobbin's Journal – *Waif to Wealth*
Poppy – *The Stolen Family*
Sophie & Juliet – *Rags to Royalty*
The Spinster – *Worth the Wait*
Holybourne – *The Magic of a Child*

A Victorian Cookbook

A Novel Victorian Cookbook-Forgotten Gems is the author's latest addition. It is full of authentic Victorian cuisine inspired by the author's colorful and classy characters from each novel. Now you can join them for a tasty meal!

Slipcases

Hand-painted by the author over 70 different impressionist style sturdy Baltic-Birch wood boxes to house her collection of seven novels. Visit KennedyLiterary.com for a look.

Paintings

After encouraging artistic reviews of her slipcases, the author has branched out to painting on canvas and wood, in the style of 19th-century painters. Visit KennedyLiterary.com and visit Carol's Art Gallery.

Links and Reviews

Visit the author's website: KennedyLiterary.com
Like on Facebook: caroljeannekennedy
Follow on Twitter @carol823599